W9-AXN-169

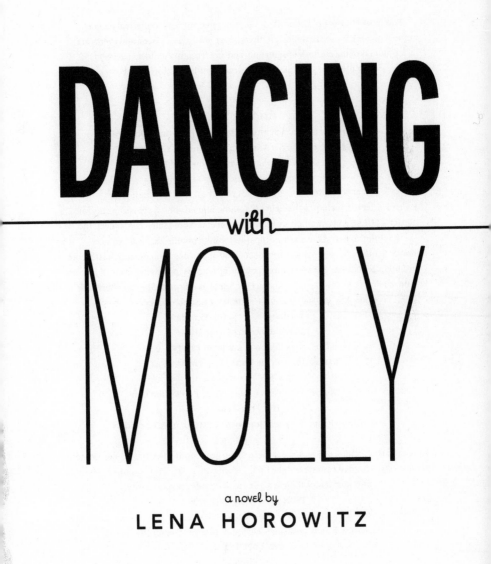

DANCING
with
MOLLY

a novel by
LENA HOROWITZ

Simon Pulse
New York   London   Toronto   Sydney   New Delhi

ᗯᗯ

SIMON PULSE

An imprint of Simon & Schuster Children's Publishing Division

1230 Avenue of the Americas, New York, NY 10020

First Simon Pulse hardcover edition June 2015

Text copyright © 2015 by Simon & Schuster

Jacket dot pattern copyright © 2015 by Thinkstock/kidstudio852

All rights reserved, including the right of reproduction in whole or in part in any form.

SIMON PULSE and colophon are registered trademarks of Simon & Schuster, Inc.

For information about special discounts for bulk purchases, please contact Simon & Schuster Special Sales at 1-866-506-1949 or business@simonandschuster.com.

The Simon & Schuster Speakers Bureau can bring authors to your live event. For more information or to book an event contact the Simon & Schuster Speakers Bureau at 1-866-248-3049 or visit our website at www.simonspeakers.com.

Jacket designed by Karina Granda

Interior designed by Tom Daly

The text of this book was set in Tyfa ITC.

Manufactured in the United States of America

2 4 6 8 10 9 7 5 3 1

Library of Congress Cataloging-in-Publication Data

Horowitz, Lena.

Dancing with molly / Lena Horowitz.—First Simon Pulse edition.

pages cm

Summary: High school junior Becca is just a "band geek" until when her friends introduce her to molly, a form of ecstasy, and she finds herself with new friends—even a boyfriend— but soon learns there is a price to her newfound popularity.

ISBN 978-1-4814-1552-1 (hc)

[1. Ecstasy (Drug)—Fiction. 2. Drug abuse—Fiction. 3. Popularity—Fiction. 4. Friendship— Fiction. 5. Family problems—Fiction. 6. Diaries—Fiction.] I. Title.

PZ7.H67Dan 2015

[Fic]—dc23

2014022175

ISBN 978-1-4814-1553-8 (eBook)

Saturday, April 26

My dad gave me this journal for my birthday last year when I was a sophomore. I couldn't even remember if I still had it or not, but I saw it when I woke up this morning. I can't believe it's just been sitting on the bookshelf by my desk for over a year now, but I remember when he gave it to me I was like, what am I supposed to write in this? Nothing very exciting ever happens around here. So, I kind of can't believe I actually have something worth writing down. I also can't believe I'm really about to write it down, because Mom and Dad would freaking flip out if they ever read it. And while we're on the stuff I just can't believe, I sort of can't believe that I'm sitting upright writing anything at all because when I woke up this morning I felt like the bottom of a shoe. It was like my head was in a vise, and I wasn't entirely sure I could move my arms. All the energy in my whole body felt like it had leaked out of my spine and dribbled onto the floor.

I suppose the ecstasy had something to do with that.

(Spoiler alert: That's the crazy thing that happened last night that I can't believe I just wrote down in this journal.)

My grandma likes to watch reruns of this old cop show on Netflix. It's called *Dragnet*, and the detective on there is always saying: Just the facts, ma'am. So, here are the facts: I did ecstasy last night for the very first time. At Jess's house. With Brandon and Pete from school, and Jess's friend Kelly. Also a fact: I am NOT the type of girl who would even CONSIDER doing ecstasy. Usually. But last night sort of tested the limits of what I consider usual. So, those are the facts.

Here's why:

Jess called me after I got home from marching band practice last night. (Yes, we still have marching band practice in April. More on that in a minute.) Anyway, she told me to come over and spend the night at her place. We do this a lot, so I didn't really think anything of it. I was especially glad that she called me because at the exact moment the phone rang, I was standing in the kitchen setting the table for dinner while Mom tossed a salad and Dad was going in and out to the deck, checking the salmon he was grilling on a cedar plank. I was really excited because after we all sat down I was going to bust out my big news:

Our band is going to the FREAKING MACY'S THANKSGIVING DAY PARADE THIS FALL.

So, I was really excited to tell everybody this, especially my mom, because she's sort of horrified that her oldest daughter is a band geek. She's always heaving these big soap-opera sighs about how ugly the uniforms are. ("I mean, really, polyester? In the twenty-first century? Couldn't they give you kids something that breathes a little?") Anyway, I was hoping that by GETTING ON NATIONAL TELEVISION with my clarinet I might put some of Mom's epic band shame to rest, but could I do that? Oh no. No, no. Because before I could get the table set, Ashley came screaming in the front door with news of her own. She was in full-blown squeal mode:

I'M GOING TO PROM I'M GOING TO PROM I'M GOING TO PROM AND I'M ONLY A SOPHOMORE.

God. It makes my head hurt just remembering the decibel level of her voice. Needless to say, my mom started crying. CRYING. Tiny tears of joy streaming down her cheeks. She and Ashley were actually hugging and jumping up and down, my mother still holding the salad tongs and flinging baby spinach across the room. I just stood there, holding the forks and watching this until my dad came in with the salmon and looked at me like, What is going on here? I just shrugged and finished setting the table while Ashley and Mom came back to earth and we finally all sat down to eat.

The irony of the situation, of course, is that I'm a junior this year and I have not been asked to prom. Not that I'd go if I was asked. In fact, it hadn't really crossed my mind that I'd even want to go. But of course Ashley has been asked as a sophomore. By Reid Boston. The freaking quarterback of the football team. Ashley and my mom talked nonstop about this the entire meal like they were in seventh grade at a slumber party. It sort of made my stomach hurt, but I choked down my salmon and salad and then just sat there staring at them while Ashley squealed on and on about Reid and how handsome he is and how he's got all of these football scholarship prospects and how she wasn't sure if he even knew her name before today.

Finally, she took a breath, and my dad looked over at me and said, How was your day at school, and I shrugged and said, Well, we found out that the band is going to the Macy's parade this fall. Even Ashley was excited by this—which is one of the reasons I can't hate her, even as much as I want to sometimes. She started squealing again and jumped up and gave me a hug and my dad was really excited and asked about all the details. Mom, of course, stayed quiet, just munching her baby spinach and smiling and nodding. Dad was trying to encourage her to get more excited for me, which I appreciate but have learned is a losing battle. He looked over and said, Isn't that EXCITING, Kathleen? And Mom nodded again and said, Oh yes. It's great. I just looked at her and said, Well, it's not a prom date or anything.

There was this awkward pause and I got up and was carrying my plate to the sink when mercifully the phone rang and it was Jess saying I should come over. I had no idea what she was planning. I didn't even know that there were other people coming. I certainly didn't think I'd be doing a tab of ecstasy. Jesus. Who am I?

This is not to say that I am a prude or something. I have a cosmo every now and then when I'm at Jess's house. She likes to make them when she forces me to watch complete seasons of *Sex and the City*. Not a couple episodes—Complete. Seasons. And her mom doesn't really care if we have a drink or two as long as we don't drive. Her mom would TOTALLY care if she knew we were also smoking weed, but we only do that when our friend Brandon is around. He and Jess used to have this weird crush thing going in junior high, but that was before Jess became the big girl in our class the summer after eighth grade. She got boobs and a lot of curves that summer and sort of never looked back.

I drove over to Jess's place in my crappy little car. I guess I should be grateful for it, but I wish I drove something besides an eight-year-old hatchback. It's just like one more thing—you know? One more way that I'm a little less cool than the other girls in my class. I feel like there are all these ways that I don't measure up, starting with my weird curly brown hair and small rack and big hips. I mean—none of these things are things I have control over. I can dress it up and I used to try really hard, but after a while it just became exhausting. All the hair straightening and eyelash curling in the world just doesn't matter when you show up in a Fiesta with a dent in the side. At a certain point, I just decided I couldn't give a shit anymore. But still, sometimes I wonder what it would be like to look like Ashley and step out of a cool car and turn heads in the parking lot. Instead I'm just this girl that nobody notices. At least when I stopped with the makeup and the outfits, the cool girls stopped making fun of me. They just ignored me instead. I was just one more band geek in jeans and a hoodie.

Is it better to be mocked because people feel threatened, or just ignored because you don't even register? Am I not even worth making snide remarks about anymore? And why do I care so much?

Jeez. I have to go get some more Advil.

Sunday, April 27

Oh my god. I feel so much better this morning than I did yesterday. My head still feels a tiny bit cloudy, but it doesn't hurt. And the muscles in my jaw and neck feel a lot better.

So, yesterday I wrote the facts about what happened at Jess's last night. I guess I should write the details, too. I'm still amazed that it happened. It all feels like a weird dream. AND, MOM AND DAD, IF YOU'RE READING THIS: THAT'S JUST WHAT IT WAS. A WEIRD DREAM. I DREAMED ALL OF THIS.

One tab of ecstasy and suddenly I'm a journaling psycho.

So, the details:

Got to Jess's house on Friday night and I saw Brandon's Volkswagen out front. How a burner is allowed to drive a Jetta, I'll never know. Brandon was there with this guy Pete who transferred in last semester. Jess said her parents weren't there because her dad had a big work meeting in Texas and decided to take her mom along. I'm not sure who in the hell wants to spend a romantic weekend in Houston. I guess Mr. and Mrs. Watson.

We were all downstairs on the big sectional in Jess's den, where her dad's enormous TV hangs in the middle of this giant entertainment center that's surrounded by books and pictures. Across the room is a big slider that opens onto the back patio, where there's a hot tub and a lawn that her mom is crazy about. I have literally seen her trim parts of the grass with scissors. No lie. Hands and knees. Scissors. She claims that new growth is too delicate for a lawn mower.

The guys were passing a pipe back and forth and smoking a bowl. Pete is supertall and superskinny with a buzzed head. His eyes were really bloodshot and I could tell they'd been there smoking since school got out. He had this dopey grin on his face and passed me the pipe. I was like THANK. GOD. And took a big hit. Jess just started giggling. She asked me if Queen Ashley had struck again, and I told them the whole story about how my gorgeous little sister, who is the exact opposite of me body wise (big rack, tiny hips, straight blond hair), is going to prom as a sophomore.

Jess knows this whole routine. She's practically been part of my family drama since we were kids. After my story, she decided that we needed drinks and jumped up to make them, but Brandon stopped her by saying, Hey, I've got something better than booze. Pete's dopey grin got even bigger and Brandon pulled a baggie out of his pocket and tossed it onto the table. Jess stopped and came back and was like, Holy. Shit. Is that X?

Jess immediately called her friend Kelly, this little Asian chick who goes to St. Theresa's. They met at this restaurant where they were both hostesses last summer, and we've hung out a couple times. Kelly looks like an anime character when she's wearing her little Catholic schoolgirl uniform. She hates the comparison, so she's got a big pink streak in her jet-black hair and most of the time when I see her she's wearing crazy clothes—like cutoff camo cargo pants and itty-bitty tank tops with sequins all over them and combat boots.

While Jess was on the phone, I picked up the baggie. My heart started racing and I felt a little nervous just holding it. There were six pills inside, each one about the size of an Altoid. They were a light green color and had little aces—like the symbol on a playing card—stamped onto them. Pete asked me if I'd ever done E and I said no and that I wasn't about to start. He just frowned in this kind of cute way and said, Aw, why not?

I shrugged and said, Oh, I dunno. Maybe the long, long line of cops that have visited our school every year since I was in fourth grade and talked about the Dangers of Drugs?

Brandon snorted. He said, Oh please. What they don't tell you is that this shit was legal until the eighties. Pete confirmed that this was true and said that shrinks used to use MDMA with their patients in therapy to help them get past traumatic events and feel better about things. Brandon said, You know those cops also showed us pictures of terrible car wrecks and talked about

the dangers of drinking alcohol and you seem to have success-
fully navigated that danger. It's just about being responsible, like
not drinking too much and jumping into a car, right?

I don't usually take advice from potheads, but I had to admit
that they were both right. I could handle a few drinks. Every
adult in my life had always made it sound like the moment I
swallowed a sip of alcohol I'd wind up a vegetable in a head-on
collision. I knew from experience that this was not the case.

As I put the baggie back on the table, I asked them what the
high was like. Pete's grin was back, and he said that it was "pure
bliss." I've heard lots of people talk about being "totally wasted"
and throwing up from drinking. I've gotten pretty buzzed before
here at Jess's place, but I've never barfed from it, and I don't
want to. But something about the way Pete said "pure bliss"—I
guess it got to me, because I've never heard anybody describe any
drug or drink like that.

Maybe it was the pot getting to my head, or maybe it was
the shit show in our kitchen at home that I'd just escaped, or
maybe it was just wanting not to be so freaking NORMAL all
the time anymore. Whatever it was, within about ten minutes
Kelly had shown up looking like a runway model refugee in
striped leggings and a gold lamé tunic, and Brandon was hand-
ing out tabs of ecstasy. Jess passed around bottles of water for

everybody. When Brandon dropped the pill in my hand, I just looked at it while everybody else swallowed theirs. Jess saw me staring at the tablet in my hand and said, You don't have to if you don't wanna.

And in that moment I realized I DID want to.

So I popped the tab into my mouth and washed it down with a gulp of water, then we all sort of sat there looking at each other for a second until Jess let out her signature WHOOP and we all cracked up.

About fifteen minutes later, we still weren't feeling anything and there was this big discussion between Kelly and Brandon about whether this stuff was bunk or not, but Pete just kept telling them to chill and give it some time. In the meantime, Jess plugged in Kelly's phone, which was filled with all this electronic dance music that Kelly's brother, Kyle, had turned her on to. Kyle is in college and is a total rave kid. He gave Kelly a whole bunch of playlists of these supposedly really great DJs that he goes to see. At first, it all sounded like music from video games to me. Lots of drumbeats under boops and beeps, and I was sort of making fun of it. But the next thing I knew, we were all dancing to it and I realized that my face sort of hurt because I was smiling so hard. Jess and I kind of danced over to each other and just started giggling. I grabbed my bottle of water when I realized I was really warm. As I was taking a big swig of water, I felt Pete slide his arm around my shoulder and say, How ya feeling?

It was at that exact moment that it hit me. It was like my stomach dropped and created this vacuum. Air poured into my lungs as I took a giant breath and I felt goose bumps shoot up from my toes along my spine into my scalp, almost like I was taking the first drop on a roller coaster, but not scary. It was like when something surprises you in a good way. It felt so great that I couldn't stand still.

I spread out my hands, which were suddenly really warm, and spun around in a circle in the den, and the lights in the ceiling and the TV screen and the lamps and the light on the patio and glowing up from the inside of the hot tub all streaked together, and I said really softly, I feeeeeeeel amaaaaaaaazing.

Pete's grin focused in front of me again and he ran a hand across my cheek. It felt like velvet and left a warm path on my skin. I could still feel it there even though he wasn't touching me anymore, and I had to take another deep breath to stop feeling like I was going to fall over. Pete raised his hands over his head and said, Not bunk, guys. This is the shit. Then he turned around and slid open the glass doors and we all followed him into the yard. I know this sounds crazy, but the music followed us too. Kelly and Jess were whispering to each other over by the stereo, and Brandon was already outside, lying in the grass looking at the stars—I think. Or maybe he followed us out. Honestly, I'm not sure. When I think about it now, it's a little bit like somebody has shuffled the cards in my head. I see snippets like snapshots, but I'm not exactly sure what order they happened in.

I remember sitting in the grass next to Pete and Brandon. I remember rubbing my hands through the turf and feeling each blade like a little kiss on my hands. My skin felt alive and my breath came in deep waves. The sky wasn't quite dark yet, and I laid back and stared up at the moon. I wasn't wearing the hoodie I'd brought over and I remember thinking that it was cool out, but I wasn't cold. There was this warmth emanating out from the middle of my chest and as I stared at the big, beautiful moon, it danced a little in the sky. I started giggling and Pete laid down on the grass beside me. I said, The moon is dancing! And my eyes are sort of wiggly. He laughed and slid his hand into mine, and it felt so good. Touching his hand was like magic. I turned to look at him, and he was staring up at the sky too.

At some point, Brandon joined us and I reached over and took his hand too. Then the three of us laid there staring up at the indigo sky, which was getting a little darker each second, and I remember thinking that I had never felt so safe. I felt like these guys both understood me even when I was completely quiet and we were all just lying there . . . feeling together.

Oh my god. That sounds SO CHEESY. But it's TRUE! I'm smiling right now just thinking about it.

After a while, I felt my mouth watering and I sat up. My stomach was sort of tumbling really fast, and I said, I can't catch my breath. Pete sat up really slowly and ran his hand down my back. My shirt was damp from lying in the grass and I felt a little dizzy. Brandon said, It's okay. Just breathe.

Pete rubbed my back slowly, up and down, and I concentrated on taking big, deep breaths. As I did, these waves of feeling sort of crashed over me. I know that sounds stupid, but that's what it felt like. I had never seen anything so beautiful as the moon over Jess's backyard, and I said so. I said, It just keeps coming . . . all this great big happiness. I feel like I'm on a boat. Pete smiled his dopey grin at me and said, That's why they call it ROLLING.

I'm not sure how long we sat there like that, but I remember hearing Jess's voice. The music was quieter, a slow downtempo song, and she was whispering from the back door: Hey! You guys! When I heard her voice, I realized I'd forgotten about my best friend, and then there she was—the best surprise ever. I said, Oh! That's Jess! And I jumped up and turned around. When I did, I saw all the lights through the windows from the back of Jess's house swoosh into view like fireworks had exploded. Through the back door I could see the big, comfy sectional, and it looked like a warm haven that I couldn't wait to snuggle up in. And there was Jess! Standing at the door! I went running toward her and gave her a big hug. She smiled and said, Feeling good? I said yes, and then I told her that my eyes were wiggly. Jess laughed and it sounded like bells ringing. I started giggling too, and I told her, You are my best friend in the whole world. We just stood there for a second, and I felt another big wave of feelings come over me. Then I told her my mouth tasted funny.

Kelly was sitting cross-legged on the floor in the corner of the sectional and she was pulling stuff out of her backpack. She'd heard me say that my mouth tasted funny and she said, Come here! Jess and I went inside, and Pete and Brandon followed us. The first thing Kelly picked up from the stuff in her bag was a pack of gum and she handed it around to all of us. It was just peppermint Extra, but my GOD. When I put the stick on my tongue, it was the best thing I have EVER TASTED in my WHOLE LIFE. The sensations in my mouth were delicious—

and it wasn't just the taste. It was like chewing this gum was a full-on sensual experience. Jess said she felt like she was having a tongue-gasm, and we all totally cracked up about that.

I put on my hoodie and felt all cozy for a minute, and then I felt hot and took it off again. Brandon said the ecstasy was a little speedy, and started jumping up and down. That's when Kelly turned up the music and all of a sudden we were all dancing. Jess scooted the coffee table out of the way, and we danced for a long time. Here's the thing about me and dancing: I don't usually do it. I always feel really self-conscious, and I'm not sure what to do with my hands. I feel embarrassed about it. But not Friday night. We danced until we were all a bunch of sweat balls. Pete peeled off his T-shirt and Brandon brought us all more bottles of water from the kitchen. Then Pete ran back out into the yard and said, You guys! Come here!

The night air felt so good—like we'd walked into a refrigerator on a muggy day. The moon was high in the sky now, and smaller than it had been before. I got goose bumps all over, and ran and jumped on Pete's back like he was going to give me a piggyback ride, which he did—running all around the backyard while Brandon smoked a cigarette. I can't believe I went running up to Pete and jumped on him like that. I'm not one of those girls. That's one of the cutesy things that girls like Ashley do, but in the moment, I had this unbridled feeling that no matter what I did, it was okay. I felt so safe—like no one would make fun of me. I felt like the truest version of myself.

When I jumped off Pete's back, he caught my hand and we raced back toward the patio and hot tub. Kelly was standing in the middle of the yard and I blinked really hard because she was surrounded by these beautiful streaks of light. Pete saw it too and was like, Damn. What the hell? Then, as we got closer, we saw that she had these glow sticks on strings that she was spinning all around herself. I sat down on the grass right in front of her, and before long, Pete, Brandon, and Jess had joined me. Jess had turned the music up a little bit so we could hear it coming through the door and we just watched Kelly spin those glow sticks. Brandon kept saying, Dude! Do you see those tracers? And yes, I did. My eyes were all wiggly again, and the glow sticks seemed to have these long tails of light that whipped all around Kelly's body as she spun them. After a couple of songs, her arms were tired and she let them drop to her sides for a second, and I started clapping. We all cheered for her and told her how amazing that looked.

Back inside a little later, my eyes had stopped twitching and we all got more gum and fresh water, but as I lay on the carpet feeling it with my hands and feet. I felt these big, slow, warm tears sneaking out of my eyelids and running down my cheeks. It was like hot syrup sliding across my face, and it felt incredible. Jess asked me if I was okay, and I said, I'm just so HAPPY.

Kelly handed something to Brandon, and then turned off all the lights in the room. It was really dark except for the light filtering in the slider from the hot tub out back. Then the music was back, and we saw this orange-and-yellow glow. Brandon was juggling three glow-in-the-dark balls that Kelly had brought with her, and they made incredible patterns in the air. As I lay on the carpet watching, I felt Pete move over next to me and take my hand again. He was propped up on one elbow next to me, and I felt his other hand stroking my face. Then he leaned over and pressed his lips to mine.

Even writing that feels weird. In the cold, hard light of day, Pete is not somebody I would ever consider kissing, but Friday night, it just felt right somehow. His lips were cool against my own, and then I started kissing him back. I've only kissed two other guys before—one was at camp the summer after eighth grade and it only happened a couple times. Then in ninth grade I made out a lot with this guy named Evan who moved in with his family next door and only lived there for a year before his dad was transferred back to Chicago. Evan was a really wet kisser. Sometimes, I felt like I needed a towel after we were done making out. He was really cute, but I have to say, Pete was a better kisser. I didn't feel like I was going to drown or anything.

I got totally lost in those kisses with Pete, but it wasn't sexy at all. I mean, I guess it was sexy, but I wasn't afraid that he wanted to have sex. He wasn't doing that thing Evan used to do when he would rub himself up against my leg, and it wasn't like we were way turned on. Also, Pete kept his hands to himself. This kissing was more about how amazing it felt to touch our mouths together. His tongue was slow and sure, and I kissed him back and started giggling after a while when our peppermint gum got all mixed up. He started laughing too, and when we looked up we realized we were the only ones in the room.

I said, Where is everybody? And Pete stood up and pulled me up, then looked out the slider and said, Wow. I looked outside on the patio and saw that Brandon was in the hot tub watching Kelly and Jess, who were also in the hot tub, kissing each other like Pete and I had been. I ran out to the patio, pulling Pete behind me, and whispered, Kissing is fun! (I don't know why we were all whispering while we were outside, but we all were.) When I said it, Kelly heard me and cracked up, pulling away from Jess, who had this big grin on her face, and said, Yeah, right?

We all wound up in the hot tub in our underwear, our feet rubbing against each other under the swirling water. I didn't realize how stiff my neck and shoulders had gotten until I leaned back against the side with my head on Jess's arm and felt all the tension draining into the steam. After a while, Kelly said she was getting pruny and we should probably not stay in too long because we needed to stay hydrated, so Jess ran in and got us all towels, and after we dried off, we all cuddled up in a heap on the sectional.

Kelly pulled the DVD of Walt Disney's *Fantasia* out of her bag and put it on. I remembered watching this movie as a little girl, but I hadn't seen it in at least ten years, and watching it on ecstasy was INCREDIBLE. The music and animation worked together in ways my brain could barely comprehend. A group of elephants or ostriches would bloom across the screen, and suddenly we'd all be laughing, and other times, tears would stream down my cheeks from the sheer beauty of it all.

After the movie, we all just lay on the couches talking about stuff. Jess brought up again how nuts it was that Reid Boston had asked my sister to prom, and Brandon burped really loudly when I said Reid's name, which totally cracked Pete up, and we all laughed really hard. Brandon said that Reid's really full of himself, and I said that meant he'd get along great with Ashley.

Thinking about that now makes me feel a little guilty. Ashley did get really excited when I told her about the Thanksgiving Day Parade, so I could've done the same for her.

After a while, I realized that I wasn't feeling the ecstasy as much any more, and looked over and saw that it was already getting light outside. I was like, Oh my god. We've been up all night. Brandon said he was getting sort of hungry, and Pete packed a bowl and passed it around. He said it would help everybody feel better as we came down, and Kelly agreed. They've all done this before. Obviously Kelly had. She came prepared with that backpack full of goodies and activities. The weed did help a little, but when we all piled into Brandon's SUV and went to IHOP I started to feel like my arms weighed five thousand pounds apiece.

The restaurant was noisy and bright even though it was only six o'clock in the morning. I never realized so many people in the world are up and around and in need of pancakes at six a.m. The waiter was named Chris, and he looked like a college student working the graveyard shift. When he came by with coffee, he smiled at us knowingly and said, So. Big night, eh, kids? Lemme get you some water.

I never thought water tasted so good in my entire life. Chris eventually put a pitcher on the table because we were drinking so much so quickly that he was wearing out his shoes getting refills. I ordered French toast and the first few bites were delicious, but then the muscles in my jaw really started to ache because I'd been clenching my teeth all night.

By the time we got back to Jess's house, I was so tired I could barely keep my eyes open while I drove home. Luckily, Dad and Ashley like to sleep in on Saturday and Mom always clears out early on for tennis and brunch with her friends. She was gone until midafternoon yesterday, which allowed me to drink orange juice and lay around in my flannel pajama pants in front of the TV for most of the day, which I desperately needed. Turns out "pure bliss" can be exhausting.

But God, was it ever fun. I get it now. I get why people call it ecstasy.

Monday, April 28

So weird seeing Pete in the hallway today. He smiled at me as he passed me and Jess. He was walking with Brandon and they didn't stop to say anything, but we all sort of shared this moment. I can't believe I made out with him.

Jess just got called out for talking in study hall. Mrs. Stone is exactly as her name implies. Jess was whispering to me, asking what the hell I was doing. She's never seen me write anything I didn't have to. I'm sure me with a journal is blowing her mind.

Ashley has been floating around the school today. I've seen her twice now. Once this morning after first period, and again when Jess and I were in line to get lunch. Reid Boston stopped by her table to say hi flanked by this tall guy with longish dark hair and ice-blue eyes named Carson who looks like a Ralph Lauren model. It caused quite a stir in the ranks of the underclassmen. Jesus. You'd think it was 1954 and Elvis had stopped by to ask Annette to the sock hop. Hasn't anything changed in the last fifty years?

This morning, when I was leaving for school, Mom blew me a kiss and said, Good luck, honey!

Good luck.

Like I was going on a game show.

She and Ashley had been talking about going shopping for prom dresses while they ate their yogurt and berries at the kitchen island. I was pouring a bowl of Froot Loops and Mom was like, There's plenty of yogurt and fruit if you want it. I know on the face of things that seems like a really sweet suggestion. But it isn't. It's her trying to control what I eat for breakfast. This has been an ongoing issue since I was in eighth grade. The unspoken message is that what she and Ashley are eating for breakfast is more healthful and will keep me slim and beautiful.

I ignored her and ate my bowl of Froot Loops and a banana, as is my custom. I did decide to dry my hair this morning instead of just going to school with it wet and twisted up in a clip, so that's something Mom can be thankful for. Probably why she said, Good luck! I'm sure deep down inside she's still holding out that I'll get asked to prom too.

The thing is, I wouldn't be opposed to prom, it's just that I feel like Mom thinks it's some sort of failing in my character that I don't harbor Ashley's princess dreams. I am pretty normal looking. Ashley is way above average. That's just the long and the short of it. I'm not repulsive or anything, I'm just your average girl. I'm okay with that. I just wish my mom was. The idea of both of her daughters in pink ball gowns heading off to prom probably has her teetering on the edge of sanity right this very second.

It was so fun not to have to worry about any of this on Friday night, to have an escape from it. Sometimes I don't realize how much time I spend worried that my mom thinks I'm a weirdo. Or maybe she doesn't think I'm weird exactly, just that she wishes I were somebody else—somebody more like Ashley. Or her. It's sort of a heavy thing. When I write it down on paper it feels like a big weight. Maybe I don't give myself enough credit for how much feeling like I'm not enough for my mom just sucks.

One thing is for sure: I didn't feel like I wasn't enough when I was rolling. I mean, I'm not going to become an E freak or anything, but it certainly lifted all of these feelings right out of me and made me feel like everything was going to be perfect always.

Tuesday, April 29

After school we had a marching band meeting to discuss continuing practices over the summer so we can be ready for the Thanksgiving Day Parade next fall. When I was at my locker dumping off my books before the meeting, I saw Jess putting prom tickets into her purse. Like it was no big deal. Just two prom tickets. Shoving them into her purse. I stood there staring at her until she looked up at me and said, What? And I was like, Um, did you just put two prom tickets into your purse? And I'll be damned if she didn't BLUSH. Yes. Jess. Blushing. I was like, Are you BLUSHING? And she shushed me. I said, Where is my best friend and what have you done with her?

I mean, Jess has sort of filled her role in our class as the big girl with the nice smile. She's that girl that all the moms at school are always clucking their tongues about and saying shit like, Oh, she's got such a great smile. If she'd lose some weight she'd be so pretty!

One time last year, Jess heard one of them say something like this in the bleachers at a basketball game and just flipped out on her. She tapped the woman on the shoulder and said, OOPS. Yep, I heard that, you skinny bitch. Guess what? I may be fat, but you're an UGLY ASSHOLE with A BIG NOSE and I can DIET. Or just CRUSH YOU. Careful where you sit.

Then she stalked off, and a group of freshman girls who had seen this whole thing stood up and started clapping. It was intense. So, Jess is pretty much her own person and couldn't give a shit what you think of her—or at least she'd say that she doesn't to anybody who will listen. So, watching Jess get tongue-tied and blush about prom tickets was not something I had ever imagined in my wildest dreams. She's just not that kind of girl; at least she wasn't until now. I guess that's one of the reasons she's my best friend: She is constantly surprising.

Jess walked me to my meeting in the music wing and spilled the beans: Her and Kelly hunkered down in a liplock in the hot tub on Friday night? Turns out not just an effect of the ecstasy. I mean, it was, but it's also . . . real. They are really into each other. Jess is always teasing about how hot some of the girls at school are, but she's also always talking about how hot some of the guys are, so I never really thought she'd be into dating a girl . . . but looking back, I don't know why not. I mean, obviously she can date whomever the hell she wants. I guess my brain has just been trained to think of girls with boys as "normal." Whatever that means. It's strange knowing that my brain has these default settings. I was surprised by my own surprise, I guess.

She told me that she felt bad when she bought tickets today because she had just assumed that she and I would either hang out the night of prom or go together, but then she and Kelly started their flirtation. (Yes, she calls it a "flirtation." Classic Jess.) Then she started insisting that I get a ticket too and come with them.

I was like, Absolutely not. For one thing I'm not entirely sold on prom as a concept, but there's no way in hell I'm going as my friend's third wheel along with her date—who also happens to be a gorgeous, tiny, Asian fashion victim who will undoubtedly wear something far hipper than anything I could ever put together.

Thanks, but no thanks.

The marching band meeting was pretty fun, actually. Lots of info about upcoming fund-raisers and packets of information on the dates of the trip next year along with sheets to have our parents sign and volunteer forms for the moms and dads who will help with organizing pledge-drive events. Pete was there with his dopey grin, sitting with the other percussionists.

He waved at me when he saw me come in, and I thought about that hand sliding up and down my back while I tried to catch my breath sitting in the grass on Friday night.

Dinner was a recap from Ashley about every single freaking word Reid said to her in the past two days. I wish Mom wouldn't giggle like she's Ashley's best friend from sixth grade when she tells these stories. It just eggs Ashley on. I don't get why Ashley wants to be best friends with Mom anyway. I mean, shouldn't there be some sort of separation? If I had a boyfriend, or a hot date to prom, I'd keep all that shit to myself.

Wednesday, April 30

One of the most embarrassing things that has ever happened to me in my life happened at school today, but somehow Jess made it better. I've always admired her not taking shit from anybody, but that went to an entirely new level today.

It was a perfect-storm situation in the hallway right before lunch. Ashley came by my locker to get the car keys because she needed to get the display board for her science fair project out of the trunk. Reid was with her and apparently he always travels with his wingman Carson, so the three of them stopped at my locker as Jess was trying to convince me to come to prom with her and Kelly again.

I was in the middle of refusing to crash her date. I had just finished saying, I don't want to go if I don't have a date and you do, when I saw Ashley pop into view, and heard Reid say, Dang. She's got a date and you don't? That's harsh.

I whirled around and saw Reid standing there with Carson. Carson frowned and said, Jesus Reid, rolling his eyes.

My cheeks were on fire, and I wanted to throttle Ashley for bringing these guys around, and strangle Jess for continuing to talk about prom. No wonder that Carrie chick burned the building down in the Stephen King novel. I finally understand that story on a personal level.

Reid wouldn't shut up though. He was like, What? I'm just saying if the tanker truck here has a date you'd think a compact model like her could get one.

Carson punched his friend in the shoulder and looked like he wanted to hit him a lot harder—possibly in the face. He growled, Shut the hell up, would you? Just lay off.

Of course, then Jess got into the mix. She elbowed me back behind her protectively and started yelling at Carson, of all people. SHE ISN'T A HELPLESS PRINCESS. SHE DOESN'T NEED TO BE RESCUED BY YOU.

At that point Reid snickered and Jess turned on him and yelled at him about being a sexist douchebag and how she was going to put her foot so far up his ass that he'd never be able to throw a touchdown pass again.

I handed Ashley the keys and she tried to smile at me and I just said, Nice. Good choice here. And she and Reid walked off toward the parking lot. Jess slammed her locker and stalked off in the opposite direction, leaving me staring after her, and Carson staring after Reid. Then we both sighed at the same time and looked at each other.

It was weird. At first we were both like, What just happened? And then our eyes sort of locked, and we just stayed there and this understanding passed between us. I felt grateful that he'd stepped in to tell Reid to shut up and it made me wonder if he has to do that a lot. If he does, I wonder why he hangs out with Reid. I mean, Reid is the golden boy of the athletics department, but still . . .

As all of these thoughts were going through my head he said, Sorry about all . . . that.

I said something exceedingly clever and winsome like, Whatever—or something equally lame, but he didn't turn and run away. He said, No really. I'm sorry. Reid can be a total dick sometimes.

I closed my locker and said, Yeah, well, he and my sister will get along famously. I said it to myself, but when I turned around he was still standing there. He laughed and held out his hand, like for a handshake, which was oddly chivalrous. He said, I'm Carson. I said, I know. Then I shook his hand, and he smiled at me.

I can't believe I'm about to write this down, but the only thing better than Carson's eyes is his smile. I know from listening to Ashley's endless twenty-four-hour broadcast of All Things Reid that Carson's prom date is this girl who goes to his church. Still, I couldn't help but think it was too bad that Ashley wasn't going to prom with Carson instead of Reid. Two jocks—a good one and a bad one—and wouldn't you know, Ashley gets stuck with the bad one.

Thursday, May 1

So after the whole debacle yesterday in the hallway, I was at home doing homework, and Jess called me on video chat. When I clicked to answer and the camera popped on I saw it was her and Kelly sitting on her bed in her room. They both finally wore me down, begging me to come to prom with them. Kelly is really funny and she kept making these droll comments about me being in a polyamorous relationship with the two of them.

I was laughing so hard that finally I was like, screw it, and said that I'd come with them just to shut them up. Jess was like,

GOOD! BECAUSE I ALREADY GOT YOU A TICKET! and started waiving three prom tickets in front of the camera.

After I hung up with them, I started thinking about Carson again. Yesterday, after we talked briefly in the hallway, the first place my brain went was that Ashley was going to prom with the wrong jock. The more I think about it, the more screwed up that seems. Forget Ashley. Why wasn't my first thought that I wish Carson had asked ME to prom? Jeez. Do I really feel so unworthy of a date to prom that I can't enjoy it when a hot boy who's over six feet tall comes to my defense in the hallway and smiles his ice-blue smile of amazingness at me?

It's not that I feel unworthy of a hot date, right? I mean, it's probably that I'm just a realist, right? I'm the conventional girl who likes the clarinet and marching band and doesn't cheat on my science fair experiments. (That display for the science fair Ashley was getting out of the trunk? I'm pretty sure my mom paid this graphic designer at her office to put it all together.) Anyway, guys like Carson don't ask girls like me to prom. Do they? I mean, obviously not, because he's going with a girl from his church, but I'm just talking theoretically. If he didn't already have a date, boys of Carson's caliber go for the pretty blond girls like my sister.

At least that's what I think. So why do I think that? Is it

one of those things like Jess announcing she's having a flirtation with a girl? Have I just been programmed to think that it's not "normal"? That somehow it goes against the Natural Order of the World for Carson to like me instead of Ashley?

Jesus. I'm a psycho. Why am I even wasting time thinking about this?

ENOUGH.

Friday, May 2

We had Family Movie Night tonight. Usually those words strike fear in my heart, because that means we have to watch whatever romantic comedy abomination has recently caught Ashley's or Mom's attention. Thankfully, it was Dad's turn to pick the movie, and he decided on this cool spy movie that was based on a novel. I really had to pay attention to keep up with it because it wasn't all stuff blowing up. It was really stylish—all about British intelligence in the seventies and eighties.

I was so engrossed in this movie that I missed a text message from Jess:

SAT: U+ME--->KELLY'S HOUSE

I texted her back and said:

I am not making out with you two.

Jess:

Fine. U R the 1 missing out. LOL.

She also texted me that Brandon and Pete are coming, and that Kyle, Kelly's brother will be there with "party favors." I told her I wasn't going to become a burnout. She wrote back:

WHATEVS.

This should be interesting.

Saturday, May 3

Oh.

My.

God.

What I have just endured is cruel and unusual. If Jess hadn't scheduled something for tonight, I might just get into my car and drive in a straight line until I ran off a bridge, or into a ditch, or straight up a mountain.

It is currently six o'clock in the evening. I have been shopping for prom dresses with my mother and sister for the past EIGHT HOURS. EIGHT (8) HOURS. We have been to TWO (2) different malls, and THREE (3) additional stores not housed in a mall.

To make matters worse, I found my dress at the first store we visited. It is a slim black sheath that comes to just above my knees. There is a short kick split at the back and the whole thing is this really fun woven fabric that looks like raw silk, so it has a sheen, but it's also stretchy, so it clings and gives in all the right places. If I'm going to endure this prom, I'm at least going to be comfortable. The dress is strapless except for this small wave of shiny sheer fabric that sort of splashes up over my shoulder. It doesn't really act as a functional strap, but it's just there for some drama and flair. It's totally sophisticated but still fun.

Of course my mother HATES IT.

She kept trying to get me to try on these big mermaid gowns in bizarre clown colors. In fact, she wouldn't even let me get it the first time we were at the store. She made me put it on hold until we'd done some more shopping. I mean, WHO DOES THAT? Who CARES about shopping? If you find the dress you want, BUY IT AND GO HOME. Mom was like, Oh no! You can't buy the first dress you like at the first store! You have to try on TWENTY MILLION OTHER DRESSES.

I was like, But why? I like THIS dress. THIS is the dress that I want.

She spent hours—literally HOURS—trying to convince me to try on other dresses. Finally, I just started doing it because I realized I was doomed for the entire day. Ashley was trying on all these gigantic gowns with sequins and feathers and bows and trains. I decided to play a game. Every time we went to a store, I'd look for the ugliest dress I could find, and go try it on. Then, when I came out, my mother would try to convince me that THIS (horrifyingly ugly) dress was the BEST DRESS EVER. SO much better than that first dress I tried on.

It got to the point that I was laughing so hard that even Ashley started cracking up. I was wearing a chartreuse mermaid dress. First of all, I should never wear any color in the bright yellow family. I have brown hair and pale skin, and it makes me look like I am dying of a rare blood disease. Furthermore, this particular "gown" was covered in rhinestones and bugle beads. It felt like I was wearing mermaid armor. Mom COULD NOT STOP talking about how beautiful it was. I finally turned to Ashley and said, ARE YOU HEARING THIS? She looked at me and we just both cracked up laughing.

I think this pissed Mom off a little, but my GOD.

Finally, Ashley settled on a dress. She is going full-bore

princess. Pink tulle for daaaaaaaaays. Whatever, she seems to be really pleased with it. Mom bitched about my dress all the way back to the first store, and all the way home. I don't care. I love it.

And thank GOD Jess planned something tonight. I love my mom. Really I do. She just drives me CRAZY, and after today, I need some space.

Sunday, May 4

Okay, I guess the headline here is that I did another tab of ecstasy. It's weird because I told Jess that I wasn't going to do any on Friday night, and then, I dunno . . . at some point, while I was shopping with my mom and Ashley yesterday, I realized that I was really looking forward to going over to Kelly's with Jess, but like in a way that was more excited than just getting to go to her house and hanging out. I think I was excited about the possibility of doing more ecstasy. This started to dawn on me when I got to Kelly's house—which, by the way, is gigantic—and saw that Brandon's SUV was there. I rang the doorbell and Kelly answered and took me upstairs to meet her mother, who is the TINIEST WOMAN IN THE WORLD. I mean, this woman is smaller than Kelly is. I didn't even know that was possible. She is very sweet, and she was setting out plates of food for us, and Kelly kept telling her she didn't have to, and she kept smiling at me and offering me food.

Eventually Kelly dragged me off to what I later learned was her and her brother's wing of the house. Yes. Wing. They have a whole wing. Their house is this big, modern thing that sort of looks like an airport. Or an airplane. It has a central entrance, kitchen and living space, a giant open room with whole walls of glass windows that go floor to ceiling, and then on the left side of the house are her parents' bedroom and offices on the upper level, and guest rooms on the lower level. On the right side of the central area are Kelly's and Kyle's rooms upstairs, and then downstairs, a giant sitting area and bar area that is really a full kitchen. There's a fireplace, and the whole back wall of their house is glass, too. It looks out onto a big pool and hot tub. The sliders on the lower level open all the way up and disappear into storage compartments.

When we got downstairs, Jess and Brandon were playing pool while Pete was mixing a cocktail at the bar. Jess looked up and saw the look on my face, which was one of the "holy shit" variety. She laughed, and Kelly acted all embarrassed. I said, Jesus! What does your dad do? Kelly was sort of sheepish, but she said that he runs a big manufacturing company that finds factories to make parts for companies like Apple and Samsung.

She told me he goes to Japan and China for months at time, and is there now.

Kelly said she had to go talk to her brother for a minute and while Jess and Brandon were shooting pool, Pete slid me a vodka tonic with a lime squeezed into it, and then made himself one. He said, Sure am glad you're here tonight. I said, Why? And then I whispered, Oh wait. Do you guys have more ecstasy? And for just a split second he frowned, and it was almost like I'd hurt his feelings. He said, Nah, I just liked hanging out with you the other night.

There was something sweet about this, but I didn't really think about it much because at the time I was disappointed that he and Brandon hadn't brought any ecstasy. I guess I'd secretly hoped that there would be some, despite what I told Jess. I took a sip of the drink, which was strong, and just as I was taking another drink I heard Kelly say, Don't drink too much of that!

When I turned around, Jess glanced over at me and then at Kelly, who was grinning like she'd gotten away with something. Jess said, NO WAY! And Kelly laughed and said, Told ya. Brandon asked what they were talking about, and Kelly said, My brother found some E. Pete frowned and said, Cool, but where are we gonna do that? Kelly told him that we could do it right here, right now. Pete asked if that wasn't going to be a little difficult with her mom around. Kelly assured him that after we went upstairs and ate all the food she'd laid out for us that her mom would retire to her wing of the house with a book and a glass of red wine, and we'd have the run of the place. Plus, she said, Kyle is in his room upstairs working on a paper he has due this week. He promised me to keep an eye out for Mom. She's generally pretty clueless.

The idea of doing an illegal drug under the nose of somebody's parent who was in the other room seemed crazy to me, but Kelly wasn't kidding. After we ate a bunch of food upstairs, her Mom thanked all of us for coming, poured a glass of wine, and headed down the long hallway, closing the door to the main area of the house behind her. Kelly's house was an awesome place to roll. It's so sleek and white. The light from the fire was beautiful and the pool and hot tub glowed outside like an alien ship had landed in the backyard.

The tabs Kelly got from Kyle were pink this time and had little plus signs stamped on them. The high was different too. It wasn't quite as speedy as the tabs we dropped last week at Jess's house. We didn't spend as much time dancing, and I didn't grind my teeth or clench my jaw quite as much. In fact, I didn't even realize I was feeling mine for a while. I was just lying on the couch in front of the fireplace for a while. Pete sat down next to me and we were talking for a long time while Jess and Kelly and Brandon played pool. Then, finally, I realized that I'd been quiet for a while and Pete was stroking his hand through my curly hair, which was splayed out across the couch. When I rolled over and looked at him, the light from the fire shot tracers out across my peripheral vision, and when I sat up, I had to take several deep breaths as the waves of pleasure crashed over me hard and fast.

This time, instead of gum, Kelly got Otter Pops out of the fridge. The cold, sweet grape Popsicle against my tongue felt like magic. We took the Otter Pops out to the pool and sat with our feet in the water. Kelly lit the gas fire feature and after a little while the guys both peeled off their shirts and jeans and jumped into the pool in their boxers. The water was heated and warm enough that they said it felt incredible. I believed them and while Jess and Kelly hung out on the outdoor furniture next to the dancing gas flames, I pulled off my shirt and jeans and stood on the edge of the pool in my bra and panties.

Even writing that sentence right now makes me blush. I am NOT an exhibitionist and I can't even tell you how MORTIFIED I would be to have anyone just stare at me in my underwear, but Brandon and Pete were both in the water, looking at me standing there in the moonlight, and Pete let out a little whistle, and I actually threw my head back and laughed. Something about this drug, I'm not even sure I can explain. In that moment, with the air on my skin, and my own curly hair sending sparks down my back as it cascaded over my shoulders, I felt . . . beautiful. I felt like my body was connected to everything around me—the sky, the stars, the water, the ground, the guys in the pool. My eyes went a little wiggly, and I took a deep breath as I felt my insides being lifted by a swell of pure joy. I was standing in my underwear on the side of a pool in an incredibly gorgeous place and I felt like I was a part of that loveliness. And the boys in the pool? I could tell from their reactions—from the sounds they were making and the looks on their faces—that they thought I was lovely, too.

I felt more than just good, or happy, or excited. I felt powerful.

I jumped into the pool and it was the most delicious feeling, the warm water sucking me in and then down. I stayed under for as long as I could and then broke the surface right in front of Pete. He smiled and wrapped his arms around my waist. I wrapped my legs around him and felt him pull me in toward him. We started kissing and his mouth against mine was even better than the Popsicle.

After a while, I heard the music wafting out of the open slid-ing doors, and splashed Pete a little, then swam to the edge of the pool and climbed out. I saw that Jess and Kelly were dancing inside next to the fireplace. Pete was trying to get me to come back into the pool, but I walked over to the hot tub instead and stepped down into it. The edge of the hot tub spilled into the pool, and Brandon and Pete swam over to it and then pulled themselves out of the pool and into the hot tub.

Before I knew what was happening, I was kissing Pete again, and then I felt another set of lips on my shoulder. Behind me, Brandon was kissing the back of my neck, and my ear, and eventually, I turned around and kissed him full on the mouth. He had some scruff that tickled my cheeks and made me smile. He wasn't as aggressive as Pete was—his kisses were definitely different.

Okay. I have to stop here and just note for the record that I would never in a million years want to make out with Brandon. I mean, Pete was one thing. Pete is sort of tall and cute and dopey. But Brandon? I don't even think he's cute. I mean, he's a nice guy, but oh my god. Am I like the easiest ecstasy girl EVER? I cannot keep doing ecstasy and making out with random dudes. I said this to Jess this morning as we were leaving Kelly's to come home and she pointed out that it wasn't a random dude, it was Brandon, who we've known since sixth grade. I know she was trying to make me feel better, but that sort of made it worse somehow.

I'm glad that we decided to get in the hot tub because Kelly's brother, Kyle, saw what was going on from his bedroom. When I turned around to kiss Brandon, Pete started running his hands up and down my body and sliding his fingers into my under-wear, and right about then, I heard a voice say, Hey, you guys. You need to chill out a little. I opened my eyes, and it was this tall, handsome Asian guy standing over us. He was really nice, and I was glad that he was there. He got us towels and we all went back inside and he played us some music—which honestly I don't remember now, but at the time I remember thinking that the tracks went together so perfectly that I would never again hear music and be able to appreciate it the way that I appreciated what was coming out of those speakers.

That's the weird thing about ecstasy. While I'm on it, every-thing seems like it's the most perfect version of itself: I'm the perfect, flawless version of me, the music playing is the perfect music, the guy (or guys, plural) I'm kissing are the perfect guys, and everything is going to be okay. Better than okay. It's going to be perfect.

I do have a headache this morning, but it hurts way less than the one I had last week. I found this forum online the other day when I was looking around for info about ecstasy and it was all these people talking about their experiences with MDMA. A lot of them were saying that the recovery time from rolling gets shorter and easier. Maybe that's true.

Still, I don't want to be making out with freaking Brandon in a hot tub. And if Pete's going to stick his fingers in my under-wear, he's sure as hell going to have to buy me dinner somewhere first. Jesus. Like two weeks ago, I'd never have even considered going out with him. And I hope Brandon doesn't make a big deal about what happened.

Monday, May 5

Funny I should be so worried that Brandon would make it weird. He's been fine. In fact, I haven't even seen him or Pete since we left English first period this morning. I did, however, just have this epic argument with Jess at lunch. Thank god we're in study hall now so she has to be quiet. Needless to say, I lost the argument. I swear I don't even know why I try when we disagree about something. It's not worth my time. She always wins. I should just stop disagreeing with her.

In retrospect, I guess it's not that big of a deal, but I really did not want her and Kelly to come get ready at my place before prom this weekend because I did not want to be there when Reid came to pick up Ashley. I just know that my parents will be on high documentary alert and there will be more pictures of Ashley and Reid snapped by my father and art directed by my mother than any other couple in the history of prom night. And I don't think I can handle it. It is just SO ANNOYING when my mom is pointing and saying, Squeeze in closer! Smile with your eyes! Let me see Hawaii in those smiles! If seventeen holiday seasons' worth of family pictures has taught me anything it's that the pain of photo sessions run by my mother could wrest information from the most hardened criminals in any interrogation.

This will be one thousand times worse on Saturday because Reid and Carson have rented a limo together and are coming to pick up Ashley after they pick up the girl Carson is bringing. The only thing worse than having to endure pictures with my mother is having to do it as the girl with no date in front of Carson. So I begged, and begged, and begged Jess, but she is insistent. She wants to come over with Kelly and get ready at my place on Saturday because I have my own bathroom. I was like, Are you KIDDING ME? Kelly has her OWN WING. But Jess just stonewalled me.

So, we're all getting ready at my house. Kill me now.

Thursday, May 8

This week has been hell. I have had a major paper or project due in every single class, and in some of them we've had final quizzes before our finals too. It's like a never-ending odyssey of complete suck. Tomorrow is our last AP Chemistry quiz, then the week is finally over. Except for prom on Saturday. Supposing I survive tomorrow.

Jess told me today that she and Kelly are coming over tomorrow night to bring their dresses so that they hang in my closet overnight and won't be wrinkled the day of. I'm going to have to get them to come early so we can get ready and get out the door before Reid and Carson show up in the limo and we all get sucked into Mommy's Swirling Vortex of Digital Picture Death.

Friday, May 9

I am now harboring drugs in my house. I cannot believe this. Jess and Kelly just left and I could throttle them both. I guess I should start at the beginning.

So, I told Mom that Jess and Kelly were bringing over their dresses to hang them in my closet tonight, and she was all excited. She's not a huge fan of Jess, but she's very intrigued by Kelly. I told her a little bit about Kelly and what her dad does, and also how cool their house is, and this was obviously a mistake because all of a sudden my mom was enthralled.

When she heard Kelly was coming by tonight with Jess, she insisted that they join us for Family Movie Night. When they got here, Mom asked them what we were planning to do after prom, and I shrugged, but Jess had it all figured out. Apparently, one of the guys on the football team named Derrick is having a big party at his house. Mom was like, Oh! I think that's where Ashley said she was going with Reid. Ashley's eyes narrowed, and she said, Yeah, I thought it had a pretty tight guest list. Jess dropped it, but she rolled her eyes at me, and I jumped in to pick the movie so we could change the subject.

I picked *Double Indemnity*, this old murder mystery, partially because I knew it would drive my mom nuts, but also because I had seen half of it over the summer at my grandma's house and I had to turn it off before I finished it, but I always wanted to see the rest. It's one of those old black-and-white movies where all the women wear tailored clothes, and the men all have hats. Sometimes I wish we still dressed that way. I was really pleased with my choice because it was one of the best movies I'd ever seen. Even Mom was won over by the end. Dad loved it and Ashley said it blew her mind.

Afterward Jess and Kelly and I went up to my room, and Kelly asked if she could use my bathroom. She was in there for a while, and Jess knocked on the door and asked if we could come in. There was a pause, and then Kelly said yes, which I thought was weird, because (a) why did Jess want to go into the bathroom? and (b) if she was okay and going to the bathroom why would Kelly say yes?

This all became clear when Jess opened the door, and I saw Kelly leaning over the bathroom counter next to the sink doing what looked like a science experiment. She had a bag of powder, a small dish, and three little bottles of colored liquid. I was like, Oh my GOD. What the HELL are you doing? My parents are going to kill me! Of course, I said this very softly. I felt like I was going to throw up. For a minute, I visualized myself grabbing the bag of powder and dumping it into the toilet, but Jess grabbed me by the arm and said, Chill out. I asked if that was cocaine, and the look on my face must've been so horrified that Jess just completely cracked up and Kelly started giggling too, but she didn't look up from what she was doing. I watched as Kelly used a tiny dropper to pull a liquid from a little bottle, then squeeze the droplets into a small dish that held a dab of the powder from the bag.

As she worked, Kelly said, Don't be silly. This isn't cocaine. This is molly.

I asked Jess what the hell molly was. Jess said it was pure MDMA. Then Kelly explained. She said, You know how when we rolled the first time, you ground your teeth and we jumped around a lot? I nodded, and she explained that was a result of the MDMA being combined with another substance like speed or caffeine pills or other stuff before it was pressed into the pill. She said ecstasy was always a different trip depending on what the MDMA was cut with.

Kelly held up the baggie full of powder with a smile. She said that this was pure. Then she apologized. She said her brother would kill her if he knew that she had lifted his testing equipment and he was home all weekend writing final papers and studying so she wanted to get it out of the house. Kyle always wanted to either test the drugs she got herself or be present while she did them. He's very protective. So, Kelly went into his phone and called his contact and bought her own.

Jess was very pleased with herself. She said, And THIS is how we're getting into the party at Derrick's. Your little sister was a total twat about that.

Of course, this made me totally crack up, because Ashley had been so snobby about the party. Then I asked when they were planning to do this molly stuff. Kelly said, You just call it molly. And I'm doing some tomorrow night at the after party. She and Jess had a conversation about whether they could get away with doing it at prom, but they decided to try it first at the after party because it seemed stupid to risk it on school premises.

I wholeheartedly agreed.

I feel weird about it though. On one hand, I'm really excited to try the pure stuff. If it's just the feel-good parts and not all the crap that made my jaw clench and caused my stomach to feel a little upset, that'll be amazing. But then on the other hand, this means I'll have done some form of MDMA for three weeks in a ROW. I'm going to go on that forum I found and look up the side effects of doing too much. I don't want to take ice cream scoops out of my brain or anything. Also, doing it at that party of all the popular kids with my sister present seems risky to say the least. I think I'll probably sit this one out.

Saturday, May 10

So, apparently it's not enough that I'm going to prom as a third wheel tonight. My mother has decided that I have to be tortured this morning as well. I have twenty minutes before the Mother-Daughter Day of Beauty begins. Usually she's out playing tennis on Saturday mornings, but today I was awakened by the sound of voices downstairs in the kitchen, and the smell of bacon. Dad was up making French toast, and Mom was standing there with a big mug of coffee, grinning ear to ear as she announced to me and Ash that she had a surprise for us. Namely, I'm being dragged out for facials, manis, and pedis at a local spa, then hair and makeup at a salon.

Ashley did a great deal of squealing. A. Great. Deal.

I know this probably sounds like I'm a whiny, ungrateful brat, but I just cannot express in words how much I do not want to be the ugly duckling on this little spa makeover day. I just know that Ash will wind up looking like a contestant in the Miss America Pageant and I'll end up looking like a band nerd with too much eyeliner.

After we ate, Mom and Ashley went running upstairs to "get ready." Would someone please explain to me how one might "get ready" to go to a spa and a salon where stylists will be paid to get me ready? I sat and ate more bacon with Dad in silence, and tried to appear pleased about this. I was really hoping to just read this morning. I found this book called *Noggin* about this guy who wakes up five years after dying of cancer and finds that his head has been attached to somebody else's body. I have a sneaking suspicion this is how I will feel once a stylist does my hair and makeup.

Dad was cleaning up the dishes, so I helped him clear the table. His French toast is a work of art. It seemed like the least I could do. As I helped him load the dishwasher, Dad said he was very proud of me. I was like, For what? And he just laughed in that way he does and said, Promise me something? I sighed and said, Okay, fine. He told me that he knew all this girly stuff wasn't really my thing, but he said he really wanted me to try to let myself enjoy it. He said, Don't wish it away, then he smiled and said, One day you'll be an old fart like me and you'll look back and wonder where all the time went. I said he wasn't an old fart and that I'd try to have fun and let Mom fuss over me a little. I guess he's right. At least I don't have to try to figure out what to do with my hair.

Later . . .

I just got home from the salon. I do not recognize myself in the mirror. I can't stop staring. I was not at all convinced that I would have a good time, and during our first appointment to get facials at the spa, I was certain that it was the most horrible mistake of my entire life. This woman poked and squeezed and scraped more crap out of my pores than I could believe. I literally had tears running down my cheeks. I felt like she was peeling my face completely off. She kept telling me to hold still and I wanted to scream HOW ABOUT I TAKE THE SANDPAPER TO YOUR FACE AND THEN YOU TRY TO HOLD STILL?

But then I thought about my dad saying to try to enjoy myself, and after a while the crazy bitch with the pokey face stick of death put down all of her torture devices and steamed my face again and then rubbed it with this really great soothing lotion that smelled like cucumbers. She covered my whole face in gauze and ran this wand thingy over it that she claimed was zapping my skin with a low-level electrical current, which probably would have been alarming had she started with that, but it just felt like little pops against my skin and after she'd almost squeezed my nose entirely off my face, I was just relieved that what she was doing wasn't making me cry.

At the end, when I joined my sister and my mom in the waiting room, Ashley looked as traumatized by her facial as I had been by mine. I told my mom that what we had just experienced was cruel and unusual punishment and she just laughed and said, Sometimes pretty hurts. Which for some reason totally cracked me up. Ash started laughing, too, and before I knew what was happening, a little woman who might have come up to my chin had me sitting with my feet in a tub of warm water and she was scrubbing my heels with what appeared to be a wood rasp. Ashley was sitting in the giant leather recliner chair next to me. Her feet are notoriously ticklish. She kept squealing and jerking and splashing the poor lady who was trying to give her a pedicure. That woman looked like she'd been sprayed with a hose by the time she was done, but Ashley had flawless "Pink Princess Perfection" on every toe. Mom and I totally giggled the entire time watching Ash jerk around in that chair, begging for mercy, and as I walked over to the manicure table with those foam spacers between my toes, I realized something:

I was actually having fun. With my mother. And my sister. Doing girly stuff.

I picked a deep red nail color called "Passion Pit" for both my toes and fingernails. Mom insisted that I get tips so that there was a little bit of length on my nails, and I didn't argue. Once we were all done at the spa, we headed over to the salon where Mom gets her hair cut.

Mom had called to make the appointments with her stylist Lynette last week when Ashley announced she was going to prom, and when I said I was going to go too, she'd called back and gotten me an appointment with one of the other stylists at the shop. I had to wait for Robin for about twenty minutes, but Ashley sat down with Lynette right away. She'd brought pictures of big swooping updos and a baggie full of dried roses the same pink as her dress and nails. I began to wonder if I was going to end up looking like a cheerleader from Texas in the 1980s.

As I watched Lynette lead Ashley back to the sinks for a shampoo, I saw a tall, handsome guy with close-cropped blond hair and biceps as thick as my waist stop at the front desk and glance down at the clipboard, then call my name. I stood up and he said, Hey. I'm Robin, and held out his hand. He had an

Australian accent, and I almost fell down. Something about him made my knees a little weak, and it wasn't just his strong grip, or his gorgeous pecs straining against the snug black T-shirt, or his perfect smile. It was the way he said "Robin." I must've looked sorta surprised because he smiled and said, Yeah, everybody thinks I'm gonna be a chick before they meet me. My boyfriend insists on calling me Rob. Let's get you shampooed.

I had a huge smile on my face while Rob/Robin washed my hair. I felt so relieved that I didn't have some old-lady stylist—like there was possibly hope that I might end up with something cool. It was worth a shot anyway.

When I got back to Rob's chair he asked me what we were doing today, and I told him I wasn't sure. I explained that I was going to prom. He asked me if I had anything in mind. At that moment, I caught a glimpse of Ashley in the mirror. She was sitting in a chair a couple of stations down and on the opposite wall of the salon. Her blond hair was teased and curled, and half of it was pinned in a wild swoop of ringlets. Lynette was pushing the dried roses in at strategic places. The whole thing looked like something straight out of a ball in Victorian England.

Rob followed my eyes, and turned around to take in the full effect. When he turned back to me I said, That's my sister. He nodded and I said, I pretty much want the opposite of whatever . . . that . . . is. This totally cracked Rob up and he paused to wipe a tear out of his eye and said, Attagirl. He ran his fingers through my wet, poodle-tight curls, which were dripping on my shoulders, and told me I have "really good hair." Then it was me who was laughing. Yeah, right, I told him. It's awful. I can't do anything with it.

Robin said I could certainly have cut bangs into it, which he was very happy I had not yet done. Then he bit his lip, narrowed his eyes, and asked if I had a picture of the dress. I did on my phone. Mom had insisted that I let her take a picture when I tried it on. She thought she'd use it to convince me that other dresses looked better. I fished my phone out of my purse and showed Robin. He smiled and nodded, then told me I had really good taste. For some reason this made me blush a little. He continued by saying that he thought we should do something simple and sophisticated—like the dress. I just said, Go for it. I trusted him completely.

I will not lie and say that it was a fun experience. Rob spent about thirty minutes blow-drying my hair with a giant round brush, which felt like it was going to tear all my hair out by the roots. He turned me away from the mirror to do the back of my head, and I briefly wondered if "simple and sophisticated" was code for "bald" in Australia. But then he turned off the blow dryer and grabbed a pair of scissors. He told me he was just going to trim off some split ends and straighten out a couple of layers to "frame my face." He made a few snips here and there and turned on his straightening iron.

Rob/Robin spent another fifteen minutes sectioning off a strip of hair, spritzing it, then clamping it between the flat blades of the iron. When he whirled the chair back toward the mirror, I gasped. I couldn't believe it. My hair was COMPLETELY straight. Not a single curl. I looked like one of those girls on TV. My hair fell in glossy layers that framed my face and flipped under just past my shoulders. Rob smiled and said, See? Told you you have good hair.

I was still so shocked that I didn't even know what to say. He said, I'm gonna put this up now in a loose French twist—I call it the Modern Grace Kelly. He gathered it all up and twisted it into a loose wrap that created a knot, which he tied up with a few hairpins. Then he told me that I could come get a blowout anytime I wanted for twenty bucks, and said, I'm going to give you some makeup now.

When he turned the chair around again, I didn't recognize myself. My eyes were perfectly lined and he'd given me a smudged silver eye shadow that wasn't too dark and gave just a hint of sparkle under my eyebrows. My lashes were curled; my

lips were a deep crimson that matched my nails. I caught my breath. Who was this creation in the mirror? Certainly not a band geek.

When I stood up out of the chair, I hugged Rob/Robin. Hard. He smiled and pressed the lipstick he'd used into my hand. He whispered, On the house. Have fun tonight.

The best part of the whole day so far? When I walked over to meet Mom and Ashley, who were waiting up front for me to get done, neither one of them realized it was me until I spoke. Ashley's jaw dropped open, and Mom gasped like she'd been smacked. Then of course both of them started gushing at the same time about how amazing I looked and neither one of them could shut up about it all the way home.

Jess just texted and said she and Kelly are on their way over.

I feel ridiculous, but I can't stop looking at myself in the mirror. I'm actually really glad we decided to get ready here now. I don't know who this girl is Carson is bringing from his church, but I can't help but wonder how she'll look. I'm feeling pretty confident all of a sudden.

Later . . .

Kelly and Jess were amazed when they saw my hair and makeup. Kelly told me I looked like a movie star. Jess made my mom write down the name and number of the salon so she could go see Rob/Robin as soon as possible, then they set up shop in my bathroom. They're in there now doing each other's hair, and I'm sitting here writing in this journal because I'm sort of bored, and as good as my hair looks, I'm worried about feeling left out tonight. I mean, I already sort of feel left out and we haven't even gotten to the dance yet.

I didn't want to tag along with Jess and Kelly because I don't want to feel like a third wheel. And now, that seems to be exactly what is happening. And what if they actually do a bunch of that molly tonight? Then I'll end up REALLY being left out. Or worse, I'll end up having to get Ashley and Reid and Carson and Church Girl to let me hang with them.

Okay, I'm going to take a deep breath and just try to remember what Dad said this morning about not wishing this away. I'm just going to put on some music and go into the bathroom, sit on the toilet, and talk to them while they get ready. This will be as fun as I make it.

Sunday, May 11

I am still lying in bed. I want to write about everything that happened last night, but before I do I must hunt down some Advil or Tylenol. My head has a bass drum it. Maybe my brain is literally blown. It is definitely figuratively blown. I. Cannot. Believe. What. Happened. Last. Night.

Especially the Carson part.

Maybe that's the drum in my head beating: CAR-SON, CAR-SON, CAR-SON.

Oh my god. I'm losing it. I have to get Advil. And water.

Later . . .

I just got back from the kitchen, where I went to get a bottle of water after I got the Advil. My mother was there on her way out to Jazzercise at the gym. She and her friend Joyce always do Jazzercise on Sundays.

Mom was very perky. Very. Very. Perky. She was full of reminders for me just now—and for Ashley, who was also in the kitchen, drinking orange juice out of the container at the fridge. It would appear that my younger sister is very hungover. Mom seems to be all business this morning, but I know that she is only acting that way to keep from sitting both of us down and trying to interrogate every single lurid detail about the night right out of us. I'm sure Dad made her promise not to give us the third degree first thing this morning.

The big reminder was that Ash and I both need to bag up our old clothes for the big band garage sale Mom is helping to organize this week as a fund-raiser for the Thanksgiving Day Parade trip. I could barely form complete sentences. Mom said we'd talk about it more after Jazzercise. Ashley said, The eighties called. They want their exercise regimen back. Mom ignored this but looked at me and said that my hair still looked amazing, even though I'd slept on it. She said we both looked beautiful last night, then she turned to me, raised an eyebrow, and said, And I'm not the only one who noticed. She said it seemed like Carson thought I looked very beautiful too.

I summoned all the strength I had left and physically pushed her out the kitchen door to the garage before Ashley could say anything. Not that I needed to worry, since Ashley was glugging more OJ from the jug. My mom was laughing really hard as I pushed her toward the car. She patted my head and said I should drink plenty of water and go back to bed, then got in her car with this big grin on her face and waved as she pulled out.

This whole thing is so bizarre—especially that Mom seems . . . somehow . . . happy? . . . that both Ash and I are OBVIOUSLY hungover. The clincher is that I didn't even have much to drink. I suppose I should write about how I got this way, but I have to sleep for a little longer first.

Later . . .

I never intended to do any of this molly stuff.

Really.

I mean, part of me was totally terrified of it. And why? I think because it was a powder, not a pill—which sounds lame even as I write it down. I mean, pills are just powder that's been pressed into a pill. Still, there was something about seeing that bag of powder that Kelly slipped into the little side pocket of her clutch that freaked me out. It was like seeing a bag of cocaine or heroin on a TV show. In my mind, doing a tab of ecstasy was one thing, but dipping into a bag of powder like a junkie or something, well, that was different. Until last night, I guess. . . .

I even said this to Jess and Kelly last night while we were getting dressed in my room. After they finished their hair and makeup we all put on our dresses. Kelly's dress was a silver spangled, sequined tube that made her look like a giant disco ball, which, she informed me, was exactly the point. Jess was superexcited about doing molly because she wanted to see how it was different from ecstasy and also because it was our ticket into the after party at Derrick's place. I love Jess and her enthusiasm for adventure of all kinds. It started when we were in eighth grade with sneaking cocktails at her house, and then smoking weed with Brandon, but something about this made my stomach jumpy.

Jess asked me how I could NOT want to try it, and I found myself telling her and Kelly about how I went online and looked up all this information about pure MDMA. As I was pulling on a pair of sheer black pantyhose with a sexy black seam up the back of each leg, I told them I'd read news stories about molly that said it had been cut with this crap called "bath salts" and how club kids in London had dropped dead after doing a "bad batch"—whatever that meant. I said I didn't want to get my brain fried at a party after prom, as I carefully stepped into my dress and zipped it up the side. As I pulled on my heels, I realized that neither Kelly nor Jess had said anything. Maybe they were really listening to my objections about this drug experiment.

I turned around and they were both staring at me, completely wide-eyed. I stopped short and looked at them and said, What?

Kelly softly whispered, Holy shit. And I realized they hadn't listened to a WORD I'd said. Jess shook her head and said she never should have invited me to prom with them. I was surprised and asked, Because I don't want to do drugs at the after party? She collapsed into giggles, yelled, NO, YOU MORON, and spun me around to look in the mirror on my closet door.

Looking in the mirror with the two of them over my shoulders, I saw what they were seeing, and I froze. I looked SO HOT. I couldn't believe it. Jess said, SEE? I shouldn't have invited you because NOBODY is going to look twice at me because you look so freaking unbelievable. And you know what? She was right. For the first time in my life I felt like I was looking at some crazy future adult version of myself. I was standing there staring at myself in the mirror like an idiot when the limo pulled up in the driveway.

Jess and Kelly wanted to race downstairs, but I stopped them and asked if we could just take a second. Jess said that she needed to talk to Reid about the after party, and I was like, Um, you cannot march downstairs in front of my PARENTS and tell him you have drugs and that he needs to tell Derrick to let you into the party. She rolled her eyes and I was like, Don't roll your eyes at me. Seriously? This was her plan? Sometimes Jess can be such a dummy. Her enthusiasm gets in the way of her common sense. Then Jess narrowed her eyes and said, OH! I get it. Then she explained to Kelly that the reason I didn't want to go downstairs was because of Carson.

I spun around and started denying that up and down, but this only made Jess laugh and she filled Kelly in on the whole situation last week in the hallway. As Kelly listened to Jess tell her how I'd shared a little "moment" in the hallway by our lockers, she did a last look in the mirror. Then she grabbed her clutch and sheer hot pink scarf that matched the hot pink streaks in her hair and took my hand. She said that Carson's date was the one who should be nervous because once he saw me, Carson wouldn't be able to look at anyone else all night. Then she smiled at Jess and said, Let's go.

I thought I might throw up as I followed Jess and Kelly down the stairs. Luckily, I'd practiced walking around in the heels Mom bought me. (Turns out small steps is the key to stilettos.) I could hear Mom already art-directing the first photographs, and I wondered if Reid and Carson were regretting what they'd gotten themselves into. As I stepped into the living room, behind Jess and Kelly, Dad turned around with the camera and just stopped and stared at me. So did Carson. In fact, the look on his face was exactly the look that had been on Jess's and Kelly's faces a few minutes earlier. He caught my eye and smiled, and I felt my cheeks flush. Dammit. I didn't want to freaking BLUSH all night long. This was going to be torture.

Mom was busy posing Reid and Ashley in front of the fireplace for the next shot, and I glanced around looking for Carson's date. I figured she must be in the bathroom off the kitchen checking her makeup or something. That's when Mom turned around, saw me, and squealed, OH GOOD, YOU'RE ALL HERE. She stopped, looked me up and down, and said, Well, darling. You look . . . so . . . grown up. Which, I suppose is as good a compliment as I could expect from my mother, considering the situation. I glanced nervously at Carson, who wasn't so much taller than I was now that I was wearing these ridiculous stilt shoes. He just smiled and said, Wow.

Jess laughed and said, Welcome to BAND GEEK BE GONE. And of course, everybody cracked up. I laughed right along with them because this whole thing was so ridiculous. Reid piped up and asked me where my date was, which was awkward because he KNEW I was just tagging along with Jess and Kelly, but because he's a total douchebag, he wanted to make me say this. I don't know what came over me, but I arched an eyebrow and looked right back at him like I owned his stupid ass and said, I am just here to chaperone these two, and pointed at Jess and Kelly.

Then I turned to Carson and said, Okay. Where is she? I had just totally put my four-inch stiletto firmly into my mouth. There was this awkward silence, and Carson actually looked down at his toes and then back up and said, Turns out I'm going stag. I felt like a complete idiot, but then the whole story came tumbling out—from Ashley, of course, who looked like she'd just floated in from a magical pink fairy kingdom in the sky.

Turns out, Carson's date (Rachel) was not present because last weekend he dropped her off at home drunk. This wasn't unusual. He, Reid, and a gang of their friends have regular parties at Derrick's place, and there's plenty of booze and weed, but this time, Rachel's parents were waiting up for her. She'd gotten a little bit carried away with a game of beer pong at Derrick's, and her mom and dad decided she was grounded for a month. Also, that she was in no way ever going out with Carson again. She can't even sit with him in church now. Carson almost didn't come tonight because he was so embarrassed about it, but he'd already chipped in to help Reid pay for the limo. Before I knew what was happening, Mom was saying, It looks like we have TWO third wheels tonight, which means that you can be third wheels TOGETHER.

It all happened so fast, I felt physically dizzy. There was that whole knee-weakening thing with Carson to begin with, which was complicated by the balance issues of wearing heels this high. I decided the best thing I could do was sit, so I lowered myself onto the arm of the couch. As I did, my short dress started riding up a bit, so I quickly crossed my legs, and it was like I had fired a gun across the living room. Carson took a step back, and I felt his eyes following the seam in my hose up up up to the hem of my dress, and then his ice-blue eyes finally found mine, and I realized that tonight was about the tables being turned: I was in charge here.

I smiled at Mom and said that was a nice thought, but I really couldn't just ditch my friends like that. Immediately, Jess and Kelly were like, Oh, it's okay. You should go with Carson! Of course, Carson hadn't said anything to Mom's suggestion, but I just waved them off, tossing a hand breezily and leaning back so I was sort of draped across the arm of the couch.

Mercifully, my dad stepped in and said, Well, we should finish up with the pictures so you all can get going. Mom insisted on arranging Reid and Ashley into three more poses, then Kelly and Jess were up for the firing squad. While they were doing ridiculous poses like Charlie's Angels, Carson walked over and sat down on the couch next to where I was perched on the arm. He said, Hi. And I said, Hi yourself. Then he said, Look, I know this is sorta weird, but . . . do you want to be my impromptu date? And I smiled my best sly smile at him and said, You mean imPROMtu? This totally cracked him up and I couldn't help laughing too. I said, Sure. But you gotta let Kelly and Jess come in the limo too. He said that wouldn't be a problem. I said he was only saying that because he didn't know Jess and Kelly very well. He thought that was hilarious too. I also said that he had to make sure we were all invited to the after party at Derrick's. He nodded, then stood up and offered me his arm. I slid my arm through his and he escorted me over to the fireplace.

My mother almost died a thousand deaths right there. She had to compose herself. Literally, more tiny tears. It was maybe the most embarrassing moment of my life. But I didn't care. Maybe I was Carson's second choice, but I was going to prom with him. Carson told Reid that Jess and Kelly were coming too. Didn't ask him. TOLD him. And the look on Reid's face was one that said he was definitely not pleased with this idea. Ashley looked completely horrified, but it was clear that Reid wasn't going to tell Carson no, especially with me looking the way I did. So that settled it, and after only another 750,000 more pictures, we finally walked out the front door and piled into the limo. As we pulled away, Mom and Dad stood on the steps snapping pictures and waving like we were leaving on a cruise to the Bahamas.

Of course, the minute the limo pulled away from the house, Jess was on Reid about the after party. Gotta hand it to that girl: She goes after what she wants like a bulldozer. Reid was hemming and hawing and talking about how it wasn't his house, and he wasn't sure how Derrick was handling the invite list and all this bullshit. While he was squirming and red-faced, and Ashley was trying to shoot me looks that said, PLEASE

SHUT UP YOUR FRIEND, I saw Kelly reach over and push the button that raised the window between the driver and the rest of us. I didn't really think anything about it until I saw her flipping open her clutch, and then it was like one of those super-slow-motion sequences from a movie where the main character is having a bad dream. I realized as she reached into her purse what she was going after, and I tried to reach across the seat to grab her arm and stop her, but she was too quick. She flipped the ziplock baggie full of molly into the air and caught it again with a gentle grab.

That got everybody's attention, and Reid's mouth hung open in midsentence. Ashley gasped and looked like Kelly was holding a severed head instead of a bag of drugs, and I realized that what had been shaping up to be the perfect spontaneous night had all just gone horribly wrong. Was Kelly INSANE? The only option for me was to just pretend to be horrified, too—for Ashley's sake—but I couldn't say anything or else Kelly might just blurt out that I'd known about it all along.

It felt like an eternity, all of us sitting there staring at the baggie of white powder in Kelly's hand. And then, slowly, a big, sly grin spread across Reid's face and he asked, Is that what I think it is?

Jess said, Yep, it's a big bag of the purest molly you're ever likely to see. She then went on to tell him that if he played his cards right he might just get to do some of it tonight, and that there was even enough to share with Derrick if he should be so inclined to let us into his after party. I was watching Ashley's face during this whole exchange, and she went on an incredible journey of emotions while she watched Reid's reaction. At first she was horrified by the drugs, and then shocked at his reaction, and then confused, and then hurt. And when Reid agreed to make sure all of us got into the after party, he put his hand on Ashley's knee, pulled her leg against his, and said, Damn, babe, this night just gets better and better!

Ashley made a split-second decision that I saw because I was watching and she snuggled closer to him and gave a little laugh that was so ridiculously cute it made me a little sick to my stomach. There were a lot of angles being worked all at once in the back of that limo, and suddenly I felt completely out of place. The power of this crazy-hot sophisticated-woman drag I was wearing suddenly seemed to be clawing at my throat, and I felt terrified. I was so scared that Carson was going to figure out how not cool I really was; that at some point tonight, he was going to come to from the haze my sexy pantyhose had put him into and see me for who I really was: an average-looking band geek with mousy, frizzy hair the color of dishwater.

Just as I thought I might need to jump out of the car at the next stoplight, take off my heels, and run back to the house, the most amazing thing happened. It seemed like Carson read my mind. He slipped an arm around my shoulders and whispered into my ear, I had a hunch you were full of surprises.

I almost blacked out with pleasure when he said that. Maybe it was his breath on my ear, but I don't think so. I'd been so nervous about this whole night—afraid that I was a fraud. But what if Carson saw me more clearly than I saw myself? What if I really am as powerful as I felt in the living room? What if I am as cool as he thinks I am—even without Robin's hair, and the heels, and the hose, and the little black dress, and the lipstick? The way Carson saw me made me feel like I was worth being seen—that I was no longer an invisible girl in a hoodie with a clarinet case.

When we pulled up to the school, Jess and Kelly piled out of the car, and Reid helped Ashley untangle herself from her very complicated billowing pink skirt. Carson and I just waited, and I took a deep breath as he climbed out and then reached back to offer me his hand. As I stepped out onto the bright purple carpet that our Jr./Sr. Planning Committee had decided to lay out on the sidewalk that led to the gym, I smiled up at Carson and he smiled back. In the warmth of that smile, I wasn't invisible anymore. I was somebody worth seeing.

That feeling came and went all night long. The other thing that came and went was Ashley's level of craziness about the whole situation. When we got into the dance, she immediately dragged me into the bathroom and hissed at me, literally hissed, What are you DOING? I just blinked at her. Honestly, it was hard to concentrate on what she meant or anything she said because her hair was SO HUGE. I just shook my head and told her I didn't know what she was talking about. She was whispering so that nobody else in the bathroom could hear us and when she said DRUGS??? it came out as more of a silent scream. I just threw up my hands and pretended that I had no idea that Kelly was coming to prom with a bag of molly in her purse.

Luckily, Ash bought this lie—for a little while at least. It gave us enough time to get back into the limo after the dance. I guess I should write down all the stuff about the dance, but my hand hurts from writing already, and honestly, the dance wasn't great. I mean, there were a bunch of teachers and parent chaperones roaming around. The music was loud and the DJ was just okay, but when he took a break there was a live cover band that some of the musical theater kids put together. They played a really great cover of "Raspberry Beret," and the dance floor got crowded in a hurry.

The really fun part was seeing people who didn't recognize

me and asked Carson who his date was. Carson got a huge kick out of this too and kept doing stuff like egging them on right in front of me. He'd be like, I know, she's totally hot, right? And then he'd introduce me like I was a girl from a different school, only when they heard my name there was always this moment of stunned recognition that was actually sort of delicious. Kelly and Jess were running around and dancing like crazy people. Reid and Ashley slow-danced to every single song—even if it wasn't a slow song. Carson is an incredible dancer, and he was wearing suspenders under his tux jacket. He had this hot little move where he'd swivel his hips and then flap open the front of his jacket, and you could see a flash of his suspenders, then he'd spin around and grab me again. It was sort of like magic. He even spun me out and dipped me during one song, sort of like a big ballroom move, and a couple of girls stopped and clapped for us.

When we all piled back into the limo to go to Derrick's party, we were all starving, so Reid tipped the driver to take us through McDonald's drive-through—yes, in the limo—and we gorged ourselves on cheeseburgers and french fries. Well, except for Ashley. Jess and Kelly kept cracking Reid up and I was glad for that because I felt like he and Jess had finally put the ugliness from last week behind them.

By the time we got to Derrick's party, his house was

already packed. Derrick had hired a couple of the sophomore linebackers to stand guard at the front door. They were under strict orders not to let anybody out to wreak havoc in the front yard, and keep things from spilling into the driveway so that the neighbors wouldn't call the cops. His parents were out of town, so he didn't want any trouble.

When we walked in the front door, it was wall-to-wall people. There was a bong in the dining room and a keg in the kitchen. You could hear the music out at the pool but it wasn't too loud. Even though it was crowded, nobody had gotten wasted yet, so it was still a pretty chill scene for the time being. Reid made a beeline for the keg and came back with beer for him, Carson, and Ashley. Carson grinned at Jess as Reid held out a beer to him and said he'd rather roll than drink. Reid got a sly look on his face, and pulled us all over to the corner and said, Okay. Let's do it.

At this point, Hurricane Ashley struck. She set down her beer, crossed her arms, and said, Absolutely not. Reid saw that she was pretty pissed and said, Whoa, babe. What's wrong? Ashley just went for it. She told Reid that her idea of a good time was not watching him roll with her sister's friends. She said that the last thing she wanted to do on her first prom night was hang out with her sister while everybody else did drugs.

It was the way Ashley spat out the words "my sister" that really got me. She said it like they tasted bad, and it was clear that Ash was pissed that I was at this party—this whole night— in the first place. At that point I was like, screw it. The way she was treating me really got under my skin. Ashley always treats me this way: sort of a practiced tolerance, a certainty that I'm going to ruin her perfect plans and her perfect night and her perfect life.

I was about to let her have it when Jess came to the rescue. For all of her "who gives a crap" bluster, Jess is surprisingly good in a crisis. She totally calmed things down by saying we didn't have to roll right away. She assured Ashley that it would only last a few hours anyway. Kelly piped up and said that she was going to start with the bong in the dining room, and Ashley huffed and rolled her eyes like this was just the most preposterous idea in the history of fun. That did it. I couldn't take it anymore. Carson was holding my hand, and I felt tall and sexy in my heels. I'd been seeing guys walk by and eye my legs all night, and watched Carson trade smiles with every jock he'd seen that silently telegraphed, Yeah, RIGHT? I know she's smoking hot. So when Ashley pulled her "I'm so much more mature than all of you" bullshit, I felt this defiance rip through me like a whip, and looked right at Kelly and said, I'm in. We marched into the dining room, and just the way Kelly and I approached the table with the bong made a path for us.

The bong was one of those big three-feet-tall numbers with glass-on-glass fittings and an ice holder so that when you pull the smoke through the water, it flows over ice in the bottom of the main pipe and you feel no heat in your lungs. Because of that, I inhaled the most gigantic bong rip of all time. By the time I blew all the smoke out of my lungs, I already felt light on my feet like I was floating over my own shoes. Kelly could not stop laughing about how much smoke came out of me, and all these guys around the table kept giving me high fives. When Carson appeared I smiled and winked at him, and he started laughing. I told the guys around the table, 'Scuse me, gents. My DATE is here. And walked over and grabbed his hand and led him past the kitchen and out through the big sliders at the end of the dining room, which opened onto the pool. All the guys were hollering and making catcalls. Jess and Kelly followed us outside and we all started dancing next to the pool.

After a little bit, Carson said he needed something to drink and asked me if I wanted anything. I told him to bring me something wet, and he laughed and headed inside. I was dancing next to Jess and Kelly and they danced with me for a second, but then Kelly danced up to Jess and got up on her tiptoes to kiss her.

They started making out, and must've gone inside, because after a minute, I realized I was dancing by myself, and maybe feeling a little paranoid about the weed.

I started wondering how I looked, and if my hair was still holding up. I saw some girls casting glances my way from the hot tub, and I recognized one of them as a cheerleader, but the other two I couldn't place. I worried they were talking about me, or that my mascara was running or something, but then I realized that I was really afraid they thought I wasn't cool enough to be at this party—especially with Carson. Part of me knew it was just the weed, and I decided to just dance more, but my toes were feeling a little pinched by my shoes. Mom's favorite adage—sometimes pretty hurts—echoed in my head and I'd started laughing to myself when I heard Carson's voice behind me: Damn, you're sexy as hell.

I spun around with my hands on my hips and rolled my eyes, a big smile on my face. I said, Where the hell have you been? I missed you.

Did I mention that Carson is impossibly tall? And that when he throws his head back and laughs, his jaw is so perfect that I just want to kiss it? He did a couple dance moves toward me and I pretended to catch him with an imaginary fishing pole and reel him in. When he got over to me, he took one of my hands in his and pressed something into my palm. It felt like a little wad of paper towel or something. I looked down at it and he said, Don't drop it. It was a piece of a toilet paper square that was balled up. I instantly knew it was full of molly. I looked up at Carson, and he grinned and held up a bottle of water. I laughed and said, Oh god. Did you? Already? He nodded and did his little spin-around dance move.

I stared down at the little toilet paper pouch in my hand. He read my mind and said, Just swallow it. Watching Carson do his little dance moves, the warm spring air on my skin, feeling floaty from the weed, and jazzed up because of all the compliments about how I looked, I realized that I never wanted to be the boring band girl again. I wanted this. I wanted this night, with this boy, and I didn't care what anybody else thought about me. I wanted to feel "pure bliss"—and I wanted to feel it with him. I thought about Pete's words for ecstasy and how molly was supposed to be so much better. Tonight was all about me, and Carson, and all the possibilities that prom had brought along with it.

I popped the little packet of powder into my mouth and washed it down with half the bottle of water. After I did, Carson danced right up next to me, wrapped his arms around my waist, and leaned his face slowly down to mine. His lips were warm and strong and slow. His tongue found mine, and thank god he had his arms around my waist because if he'd made my knees weak before, this time, he took my legs right out from under me.

I'm not sure how long we kissed, but I didn't care who saw. I was lost in it when Jess came running up with Kelly. Both of them had a couple of water bottles, and I could instantly tell from their excitement that they were anticipating their own molly hits kicking in at any second. Reid and Ashley were right behind them, and their energy was remarkably different. Jess was telling me how much I was going to LOVE this high, and Ashley pushed in next to me and stared daggers at me. She was hissing again: I can't BELIEVE you did this. I should tell Mom and Dad the minute I get home.

I just smiled at her. In that moment, I honestly didn't care what she did. Reid was looking pretty glum, and for the first time all night he sounded kind of impatient with Ashley. He said, Jeez. Chill out. It's probably gonna be a really fun time.

Ashley whirled around and told Reid that if he did any molly he could just take her home right this second. He held up both hands and got a little sheepish. He told her he wasn't going to, but I could tell he was miserable to miss out on this. Ashley tried to make things better by grabbing his hand and leaning in to kiss him.

I'm not sure how long we danced after that. I think it was around midnight when we dropped, and I know it was getting light outside when we all got out of the hot tub and started to go home, so it probably lasted about five hours? But . . . wow.

What.

A.

Five.

Hours.

Carson and I were dancing and he untied his bow tie so it dangled down on both sides of his collar like he was a sexy movie star or something. Then he reached up and undid a couple buttons on his shirt. I don't know what came over me, but I reached my hands up and started undoing all of the buttons on his shirt. I wasn't feeling the effects of the molly yet, but I felt bold. Being there with him, and looking the way I did, just changed me on the inside. I felt like the whole evening had culminated in me being this sexy, wise woman—not a girl but a woman. I felt older than I actually was. Or maybe I just felt independent from all the ways that I'd always considered myself to be just another lame high school girl—boring and predictable.

Once I unbuttoned Carson's shirt, his pecs and abs peeked out from the panels of his shirt, which were held in place by his suspenders. I ran my hand across his chest and down his sexy stomach to his belt buckle and pulled him toward me. He kissed me again, and I felt him shimmy out of his jacket. He tossed it over the back of a nearby deck chair, and he pulled his suspenders down, so they looped across his hips and hung there while we danced.

We kissed and danced for a long time, and then the light from the pool started drifting up—like the air was ignited by this bright haze of light. The whole backyard seemed to be glowing. My eyeballs started to twitch a little, and then it felt like I got hit by a g-force—like when Jess peels out in her car too fast, and I get tossed back against the seat. Only this feeling didn't make me fear for my life. These feelings were like a full-body massage of the warmest, firmest variety. Carson felt it too, and he held me close and whispered that I should just breathe with him. And we did. Every time he breathed out, I breathed in—like I was breathing him in. Our bodies were pressed together so tightly I could feel every inch of him against me, and as the lights swirled in tracers around me, the music beat from somewhere inside me, like it was being produced someplace just behind my sternum and radiating out of my body, into Carson's, then reverberating out to the entire party.

This was a different high than regular ecstasy. The molly was not speedy or jerky. I wasn't chewing on my own tongue, and my stomach didn't hurt at all or feel all gurgly the way it did before. This was just like being on a really intense boat ride—lots of waves, lots of high pressure flooding my body and pressing against me.

At one point Carson grabbed his jacket and pulled me away from the group. We went inside and found a couch in Derrick's front den. It was pretty deserted at that point—or at least, I don't remember anyone else being in the room; just me and Carson. We sank down onto a couch and kicked off our shoes. Carson pulled me on top of him and we just started kissing. We must've kissed for a long time. For a while, I felt like if I stopped kissing him I would come unplugged and my whole body would power down. His fingertips against my skin created these tiny hot spots wherever he touched me, and when his hands would move to another area, those hot spots would glow and then give me goose bumps all over.

I'm not sure how it happened, but Carson wound up wearing just his boxers on the couch. I was kissing him all over his shoulders and chest and stomach. And he was stroking my arms and legs and back and face with his fingers. It's weird to write this down, but it wasn't about having sex at all. It was more about the sensations, the feelings between us—it was just me and him, and no one else in the entire world.

Eventually, we left most of Carson's clothes and my shoes in a pile and somehow made it out to the hot tub. The house was mainly deserted now. On the way, we passed the kitchen, where Reid and Ashley were sitting at the bar. Reid was drinking beers and looking miserable. As Carson led me past them, I smiled because I felt so happy to see them both. If Ashley's eyes were weapons they would've killed me. Reid asked Carson something about how he was feeling, and Carson said something about how incredible this was. Ashley didn't even speak to me, but I didn't feel angry or worried or guilty, I just felt . . . love for her. That sounds so clichéd and cheesy. The best part of a pure molly high is that the feeling of not being enough, of not being cool, of being "less than" everyone around me just disappears.

Outside, Jess was so excited to see me when we got to the hot tub. I unzipped my dress and tossed it over on a deck chair and slipped into the warm water next to Carson, who was still in his boxers. He wrapped an arm under my head, and I lay back against him. I felt so much love for everyone around me.

Derrick got us some waters, and convinced Reid and Ash to come outside. They kicked off their shoes and put their feet in the water. Ashley's hair was sagging in lots of places, so she pulled out all the dried flowers and lined them up next to the hot tub, then pulled out all the bobby pins one by one. I think it looked better down once she got all that crap out of it.

As I looked up at the sky and saw the sun rising, Jess announced that she wasn't feeling anything but hungry anymore. I guess we'd all pretty much come down at that point. We all dried off and slid back into our clothes. Carson and Reid joked about the walk of shame while Reid called us a cab big enough to get us all back to Reid's house, then he and Carson took us all home.

I didn't sleep right away. I've been drinking water like a camel in the desert. I feel like I got a little dehydrated, but I don't feel nearly as bad as I did that first time I took ecstasy. Molly is definitely a better high. I'm a little achy, but it was so completely worth it for those five hours with Carson. It really was pure bliss. I felt like I was invincible, like I could understand anything and love anyone.

Monday, May 12

I'm sitting in first period. My English teacher, Miss Sloan, thinks I'm taking notes, but I wanted to write down what just happened.

On the way to school this morning, Ashley wouldn't even talk to me, which . . . whatever. I was still feeling a little tired, so I decided just to let her have her space. I'm done feeling guilty for feeling good. She can make her decisions, and I don't judge her for them. What I couldn't shake as I drove into the parking lot was the fear that Carson wouldn't even talk to me today. My head started to hurt a little as I sat in the car after I parked. Ashley had gotten out in a huff and walked into the building already, and I just sat there sipping coffee out of my travel mug. What if Carson was just into me when I looked the way I had on Saturday night? I had gotten up a little earlier than usual to put on some eyeliner and lipstick, but my hair was back to its usual curly mess.

Ugh. Is that what it's like now? All my insecurities come racing back into my head when I'm not on molly? That's lame. Where's the girl who unbuttoned Carson's shirt while dancing out by the pool? Anyway, as I was sitting in the car wondering how I was going to make it through this day if Carson ignored me, I had a little breakthrough. Worrying about Carson was stupid. If he was going to ignore me after the great time we had, I shouldn't give him a second thought. It made my stomach hurt, but I pushed through it and got out of the car, grabbed my clarinet and bag, tossed my purse on my shoulder, and marched into the school with my head up.

When I turned the corner into the hallway where my locker is, I saw Jess first. She was unloading her backpack and talking to

Carson. He was actually leaning against my locker. When he saw me, he gave me the biggest smile over Jess's head, and it made me smile automatically. He hadn't forgotten, and he wasn't a douche. He was actually a nice guy, and we'd had a nice time.

Jess whirled around and saw him staring at me, then looked back at me with a big, mischievous grin on her face. She said my makeup looked hot, and I blushed a little and told her she wasn't supposed to point it out in front of Carson. She laughed and said, Him? Oh, he's just hanging around to ask you out this weekend because he's got a mad crush on the hottest band geek in school.

She slammed her locker and left before I could yell at her.

Carson was laughing, and I told him that I needed to get into my locker. He said I'd have to pay the toll. I asked him how much that would cost me. He said, One kiss, and a date on Friday night.

Then he leaned down and gave me a sweet little kiss on the lips right there in the middle of the hallway.

I almost fell down. I couldn't believe it. Is this my life now?

As I put my stuff in my locker and grabbed the books I needed for English, I asked him if he was serious about the date on Friday. He asked why he would joke about something like that. I just shrugged and told him that if it was just going to be us, Jess wouldn't be there. There'd be no molly. Carson frowned and put his thumb under my chin and gently directed my face up to look him in the eyes. He said he wasn't into my drug hookups. He was into me.

He says he just really wants to hang out with ME.

Why is that so hard for me to believe? I mean, why shouldn't he want to just hang out with me?

Friday, May 16

I marched my legs off in band practice this week. I think Mr. Peterson is nervous we're going to slack off during the summer, so he's been like a freaking slave driver.

At least the marching has taken my mind off this whole date with Carson. We've seen each other every day at school, and eaten lunch together with Jess and Kelly and sometimes Reid and Ashley—although Ashley has only let that happen twice. I think she's still pissed about the other night. Anyway, I'm still nervous about being out alone with Carson. Without everyone else around to help carry the conversation, I'm going to be this really lame, boring person.

I know that the whole point of tonight is for us to spend some time getting to know each other, but I sort of wish there were going to be other people on the date. I especially wish that Molly were coming. (Oh god. That's so lame that I just used the name of the drug like it's the name of a friend.) Is that the way I really feel? All I know is that I wish I could feel all the time what Molly makes me feel when I'm rolling. Maybe not the visual stuff like the eye twitching and the light tracers. I just wish I felt as confident and bold and sure of myself. I'm afraid I'll be a tongue-tied idiot when Carson comes to pick me up.

Mom is way thrilled that I'm going out with him again. She tried to hug me and jump up and down in the kitchen and squeal like she did with Ashley. I was like, Um, absolutely not. She begged me to bring him in when he gets here, but I made him promise me that he would just text me from the curb.

I just think that molly makes it easier for me to relate to people—at least to a hot guy like Carson. I suppose I shouldn't need outside help with that. Ashley sure doesn't. But she's used to being pretty and popular and all that jazz. This is insane. I know I can't go around rolling on molly every time I want to go on a date. I logged on to that online forum and read all these posts by kids who did molly at their actual proms—not the after parties, but actually at their schools DURING the prom. It was crazy to read about it, but I get it now. I understand why it's something that people do. There is this one girl who was all high-and-mighty and judgmental. She reminded me of Ashley. She was posting all these links to articles about this guy in London who was nineteen and died of a "bad batch" of molly. It was all over the news, and the *Guardian* had several big articles about it.

Still, most of the other people on the forum posted about how those stories are few and far between, and most of the other deaths attributed to molly (or just ecstasy) are because people don't get enough water and get dehydrated. I would never be dumb enough not to drink enough water. And Kelly always tests the stuff that we do, so we'll never have to worry about a "bad batch"—whatever that means.

I'm so nervous. I'm so nervous. I'm so nervous. I'm so nervous. I'm so nervous.

I wonder if it'll change when I see him? Like on Monday at my locker, when I saw Carson there talking to Jess, all my nerves just disappeared.

I'm going to go check my hair and makeup one more time before he gets here. When I got home from band practice, I took a shower and tried to blow my hair out straight. It sort of worked. It's not nearly as sleek as when Robin did it at the salon, but it's not frizzy, which is a step in the right direction.

Saturday, May 17

Last night was not a total disaster. I mean, it definitely got off to a rough start, mainly because I felt completely tongue-tied with Carson. It wasn't too big a deal because we were going to dinner and a movie. We got burritos at Carson's fave burrito joint. It's not superfancy or anything, but he told me the restaurant serves sustainable and humanely raised pork, beef, and chicken products, and it was nice and casual. At least we didn't go to some fine-dining establishment where I would've worried about which fork to use with which course. These burritos came wrapped in silver foil, and we ate them with our hands.

Still, I felt . . . awkward just hanging out with Carson. I wore cute jeans that I think make my butt look good, and some little silver flats with a V-neck T-shirt and a bra that keeps everything lifted front and center. I caught him staring a couple times, which is a job well done on my part. But he wasn't gross or anything—I mean, he can definitely hold eye contact, and maybe that was the problem: Carson is so good-looking that he sort of takes my breath away.

So he kept asking me questions and I'd just catch myself staring at his perfect eyes, or his perfect jawline, or his perfect nose, or his perfect lips, and then he'd say, Yo. Everything okay?

And I'd blush and take a big bite of my burrito and then

ask him to repeat the question with my mouth full of food, and then blush worse because I was talking with my mouth full, then hold up a finger and finish chewing and swallowing and then ask him to repeat the question again, and then, while he was talking, I'd get distracted by his eyes, or his nose, or his lips, or his jaw AGAIN . . . and . . . well. Yeah. So that's how the whole meal went.

The movie was just okay. It was based on one of those books where the world is a dark and gloomy place and impossibly gutsy girls and impossibly handsome boys fight battles to the death to outsmart evil alien overlords. Somewhere in the middle of the film, Carson jumped when one of the evil alien over-lords dropped out of an elaborate set of twenty-second-century ductwork in the core of a spaceship that was housed in a grain silo somewhere in Nebraska. (Yes. Nebraska is apparently where the alien overlords will set up their silo-hidden space fleet in the coming nuclear winter.) Carson jumped so high that I think his entire body came off his chair in the theater.

For the first time all night, I felt the tiniest bit brave, and stopped wishing I had the chemical courage of a dose of molly for just long enough that I was able to reach over and grab his hand, which was white-knuckling the armrest. And you know what happened? He glanced over at me, smiled, and whispered, Thanks!

After the movie, we were mostly quiet on the way home. Carson put his car in park by the curb about a block away from my house. He asked if we could talk and I said yes. Then he asked me if anything was wrong. I'm not sure what came over me, but I decided to just be completely honest with him. I told him that I feel like I'm just really bad at going on dates—especially the conversation part. He said that I wasn't bad at it when we went to prom, and I told him that was because I didn't have a week to be nervous about it. It just sort of happened that night—and then we danced, and had the pot and the molly to help me relax.

He reached over and put his hand on my leg, and kissed me, first just a peck, and then I leaned into him again and we kissed for a long time—until the console between the front seats started digging into my side, and I guess something wasn't sitting so well in his pants because he was digging at his fly for a second, and whispered, Damn, girl. You got me all riled up.

I laughed, and he smiled at me and grabbed my hand again. That little moment—where he wasn't afraid to laugh at himself—made me say something else. I blurted out: I've just been nervous all night that you don't like me.

He just shook his head and looked at me like I was crazy. He said, How could I not like you? Then he explained that if he didn't like me he wouldn't be here, and told me that he wasn't into playing games. He said he was relieved that we'd talked about it because he was afraid he'd been turning me off all evening. I practically yelled NO! at him, and assured him that he was one of the sexiest human beings on the planet. I couldn't believe that HE was worried about ME liking HIM. I mean, in what world does that happen? As if I could EVER not like him. . . .

I told him I was sorry I had been so weird and the conversation had been so screwed up over dinner.

He leaned over and kissed me again, long and hard on the mouth. I leaned into him and kissed him right back. His tongue on mine still tasted like peanut M&M's from the movie theater. He whispered, Conversation is overrated anyway.

I have to say that I completely agree.

Sunday, May 18

So . . . I was just in the middle of texting with Carson. He sent me a text that said:

Thinking about you.

Then another one that said:

Thinking about kissing you.

Then a third one that said:

Let's do more of that.

I was about to text him back when Ashley came into my room and closed the door behind her, like she was being chased. I asked if everything was okay, and she looked haunted, like she was afraid to walk across the carpet in my bedroom because it was actually not carpet but a pool of acid that might eat away her feet if she moved from the door.

Finally she ran over to my bed and jumped on it next to me like she was a little kid. She had this weird, guilty look on her face. I mean, I don't know what else to call it. She looked like she had eaten a whole cake or broken a window or something. I told her to hold on a second so I could text Carson back. Just as I was about to press send on a text that said:

More kissing could be arranged. . . .

Ashley blurted out something I never thought I'd hear her say: I want to do ecstasy. Or molly. Or whatever you call it.

I just stared at her and blinked, and forgot all about the text I was going to send. Ashley immediately started explaining in a low voice that Reid had been bitching and moaning ever since prom about how he didn't get to roll with us, and putting pressure on Ashley to roll with him at the school's graduation party, where everyone stays in the school and gym so nobody kills themselves drinking and driving around to parties.

Anyway, turns out Reid is really keen on Ashley rolling with him at this party (which, I think sounds like a TERRIBLE idea—rolling at a school-sponsored party), and so she started quizzing me about ecstasy and molly, and what the differences were. I told her all that I knew about it—just that ecstasy was usually cut with something and that molly was supposedly "pure" MDMA, which Kelly tested to make sure of with her little kit.

I told Ashley about how I felt when I was on ecstasy. She thought maybe it made you trip and see scary stuff, like acid would. I told her that the only visual stuff I'd experienced was pretty—like lights dancing around—and that coming down was no fun the first time, but that it had gotten easier since then. Also, that coming down from molly didn't seem like a big deal at all.

Ash asked if I was nervous about it hurting my brain or

dying, so I showed her the online forum I'd been reading, and she lay on my bed and read several of the threads. Then she asked me point-blank if it was "fun." I told her that molly was more fun to me than regular ecstasy. I said that when I was high on molly I felt the way I'd always wanted to feel: confident, pretty, in control; like I loved everyone, even people I normally didn't like very much, and also like everything was going to be all right.

After a while she closed my laptop and nodded. She told me she wasn't sure if she wanted to do it or not. Suddenly I was the one who felt guilty. It's one thing for me to do drugs, but it feels like a completely different thing to encourage my little sister to do them. I told her that she shouldn't let anybody pressure her into doing anything—especially not Reid. I don't think she took that very well, because she sort of narrowed her eyes at me and huffed out of the room.

I can't help it. I think Reid is a big tool.

I hit send on the text to Carson after Ashley left my room. He wrote back immediately:

YEHAAAW!

Which made me LOL.

Wednesday, May 21

I told Carson that Ashley asked me about molly because Reid was trying to get her to do it at the graduation party. He told me that Reid had been talking to him about the same thing. The whole thing snowballed when Ashley and Reid joined me and Jess for lunch. Of course, Jess thinks it's the best idea in the world, and immediately said she'd ask Kelly about getting some. I tried to put the brakes on the idea of doing drugs at a school-sponsored event, but when I did that, Ashley took it as her cue to act like I was trying to tell her not to do molly, and started insisting that she wanted to.

I pointed out that maybe it wasn't the best idea in history to be blissed out in the middle of a party where there were going to be a bunch of teachers chaperoning and it was right in the middle of that sentence that Pete and Brandon showed up and sat down next to us. When they got wind of what Reid was planning to do they were all for it and told Jess that they wanted in on the action too. I mean, I love doing molly and all, but am I the only person who thinks this is a bad idea?

Carson was waiting for me after band practice today. He and Reid were hanging out in the parking lot next to my car. Ashley was draped over Reid like a jacket and the three of them were talking about how much fun it would be at the party. Reid and Carson don't have to worry about coming back to school anymore because they're seniors, but Ashley and Jess and I could get in a lot of trouble if we got caught.

After I said that, Reid looked at me like I was trying to run over a puppy with my car and started assuring Ashley that he and Jess and Carson would make sure that nothing would happen to her. I didn't want to start a big fight or anything, but I asked him how exactly he could guarantee that, seeing as he'd never done molly, or even ecstasy, before. That's when Jess came running up and said that Kelly had texted her with news: Kyle, Kelly's brother, is spinning at this big underground after-hours party on Saturday night in a huge warehouse downtown, and he's going to put us all on the list.

The minute Reid heard this, he was all in. He told me that we'd "practice" doing molly at the party this weekend and see how it went, and that way we'd be "prepared" for the graduation party. Ashley seemed to think that this was a great idea. Jess said Brandon and Pete were a go for the party this weekend, too. My only hope is that Ashley will just not like it that much and I'll be able to talk her out of rolling at the graduation party, but something tells me that's not going to happen. If she's anything like me, she'll love doing molly.

I can't help but feel like this is going to get out of control.

Friday, May 23

Carson and Reid came over for dinner tonight. Mom was in heaven. She was in "coolest mom ever" mode and prepped Make Your Own Pizza night. I think she may have flirted with Reid and Carson more than Ashley and I did. Dad came home from work as we pulled the first round of pizzas out of the oven and jumped in on the fun too. I have to admit, I had a good time— even though it was Ashley's turn to pick out a movie and she chose *Sleepless in Seattle*. Usually that movie drives me crazy, but I actually didn't mind it this time. Maybe holding hands with Carson while I watched it helped. I guess ultra-romantic movies aren't so bad if you feel like it's possible to have that kind of romance off-screen.

After the guys left, when I was getting ready for bed, Jess texted me. She said that Kelly couldn't get molly for the party tomorrow, but that her brother had scored some ecstasy. I feel so bummed about that. I mean, ecstasy is fun, but the molly that we did after prom was so much better. Also, I have this nagging feeling that I'm going to be worried about Ashley the entire time and not really able to enjoy myself or Carson or the music as much as I want to.

Oh well. I guess we can just try it tomorrow night and see how it goes. At least Kyle will be there. He told Kelly that he'd keep an eye on all of us. Still, I hope there aren't any problems. Jeez. When did I turn into such a nervous Nellie? Who am I kidding? I'm going to roll tomorrow night and have a blast with Carson. I'm sure Ashley will have just as much fun with Reid. It's not like we're shooting heroin or something. What could go wrong?

Sunday, May 25

Wow. I just read the last words I wrote in this journal. If that wasn't tempting fate, I don't know what is. Note to self: Never write "what could go wrong" in a journal. The next entry will be horrifying.

Pretty much everything went wrong last night. I feel like crap—and not just from the ecstasy. Of course, that's really where everything started to go bad. Kyle got these little red tablets that had lightning bolts pressed into them. Brandon, Pete, Jess, and Kelly had just dropped when Carson, Reid, Ashley, and I arrived, so we'd barely gotten inside the door of the party before Jess was passing around the tabs and water bottles. Ashley didn't even hesitate, she just gulped hers down and I followed suit so that we'd be on the same wavelength at least and I could sort of track what she was feeling.

At first we didn't really feel much. The warehouse was

huge, and there were these totally ripped shirtless guys and girls in bikinis dancing on big cubes all around the dance floor. Kyle waved to us from the DJ booth and we went over to say hi. He told us to "enjoy the lightning" and then we all started dancing. This ecstasy took longer to hit than the other two times, and once it did, it was not nearly the same as the molly. In fact, it was awful at first. My stomach got really upset and I was grinding my teeth and clenching my jaw like crazy. It was really speedy and it made me feel jittery. My eyes twitched so much that Carson grabbed my hand and took me outside where Pete and Brandon were. They were smoking cigarettes, and I sat down for a while, but being away from Ashley made me nervous because I kept thinking about her and wondering if she was okay. I got really paranoid, so Carson brought me back inside to find Ashley.

I shouldn't have been worried at all. By the time we got back inside, Reid was shirtless, and he and Ashley had climbed up onto one of the boxes with one of the girls in the bikinis and were dancing with her. Ashley saw me and squealed, then threw her hands over her head and danced like a maniac. I just started laughing because she looked like she was having a really good time, and I finally started to relax. Jess and Kelly came around with water and Blow Pops. Having that sucker helped me stop clenching my jaw so much and it tasted amazing.

We all started dancing together around the big box that Reid and Ashley were on. My sister looked amazing. Kelly had sprayed body glitter all over her, and her blond hair was catching the black lights, and for a while it looked like she was shooting lasers out of her head, creating these beautiful patterns. She saw me looking up at her and pointed at me with a big grin on her face. She jumped off the box and came running over and threw her arms around me.

Ashley has never been one for public displays of affection, but somehow it seemed exactly right. She kept telling me thank you over and over again. I asked her for what, and she said, For this AMAZING NIGHT. I feel SO GOOD!

Ashley danced near me and Carson for a while, and then Reid jumped off the box and started kissing her. Ashley just melted into him, and I realized that's exactly what I wanted to be doing. I turned around and saw that Carson had slipped off his T-shirt and tucked it into the waist of his jeans. The whole warehouse was packed now, and we all seemed to be moving and dancing and grinding and breathing at the same time. The lights bouncing off his chest made him glow, and the speed in the ecstasy made my eyes twitch so fast that Carson looked like a big ball of pink, purple, and yellow light. I was feeling a little dizzy, so I reached out to touch him. My hand landed on his chest, right over his heart, and I swear I felt it pounding there against my palm.

Carson had his head thrown back and his eyes closed, completely lost in the music. When I touched him, his face lit up, his eyes fluttered open, and he got the biggest grin on his face. He stopped dancing and folded his hand over mine, then pulled me toward him and held me close against his body. I could feel him taking deep breaths, and as his body rose and fell against mine, he leaned down and kissed me.

Our mouths locked together, and our arms pressed our bodies into each other so tightly that for a little while, it felt like we had combined ourselves. I felt like our skin had merged, and we were breathing together as we kissed—each inhale a gift, each exhale a revelation.

I felt another mouth on my neck, someone else's breath on my ear. I pulled away from Carson, breaking the spell, breaking our moment. I turned and saw Brandon behind me. I felt his breath on my face as he leaned in to try to kiss my mouth. I tried to push him away, but he kept pulling me toward him. I heard Carson yell, WHAT THE FUCK, DUDE? And saw his fist shoot out past my face and knock Brandon in the nose.

The blood that sprayed out of Brandon's nose caught the

light and was sort of beautiful, but it was only beautiful for about a split second, before he crumpled to the floor next to the big block, knocking into Ashley and Reid, who stopped kissing and turned around just as Carson lunged onto Brandon and hauled back his fist to hit him again. I heard someone yell NO! and realized that it was me. Suddenly Pete materialized out of thin air and tried to pull Brandon to his feet as Reid jumped in and held back Carson's arm, which was ready to fly toward Brandon's head again.

Damn speedy ecstasy. I guess this is what those kids on that forum were talking about. They mentioned that every once in a while the balance of the MDMA to the caffeine or speed, or whatever they cut it with, is seriously off. I still can't imagine anybody throwing a punch while rolling on molly, but maybe ecstasy just affects people differently. Or maybe Carson would have hit Brandon for trying to kiss me stone-cold sober. Whichever, it happened, and all the guys were yelling at each other, while Ashley stood there, wide-eyed, her jaw clenched, her arm wrapped around her stomach like she was going to throw up.

I went over to her and hugged her and told her it was going to be okay, and Jess came over to us and said, Let's go get some air. She and Kelly were leading the way toward the door when

we saw the big metal door of the warehouse fly up and red-and-blue flashing lights. These weren't part of the light show. They were coming from a cop car and an ambulance. Jess and Kelly stopped dead in their tracks as two paramedics and a cop started shoving their way through the crowd toward us. I was so confused. Ashley yelled over the noise, Did you call the COPS? And I was about to say NO when they pushed past us, and we turned to see them move past Carson, Reid, Pete, and Brandon, who was standing there with his head back, holding his T-shirt up to his nose.

It was only then that I saw a circle had cleared on the other side of the block where Ashley and Reid had been dancing. There was a girl with dark hair lying on the concrete floor. As the lights swept across her, I could see that she was twitching, violently, her mouth covered with a weird white liquid that seemed to bubble up from inside her. Soon, the paramedics and the cop surrounded her, and Jess appeared in front of all of us and shouted, LET'S GO! NOW!

Jess grabbed Kelly by the hand and cleared a path through the crowd, pushing and shoving people out of her way. We muscled our way past the DJ booth, where Kyle was still spinning, headphones on, lost in his own music. Finally we hit the cool air of the outside, and we started running.

We didn't stop until we were back at our cars.

Everybody except for Pete and Brandon went back to Kelly's house after we left the club. Kelly and Carson drove everybody, and I didn't really grasp until yesterday morning when we all woke up sprawled across the couches and carpet what a truly terrible idea it was for ANYONE to be driving.

I thought Ashley would be totally freaked out, but after we got back to Kelly's we all tried to relax in the hot tub and Kelly passed around a little bong she had packed with some really good weed. It helped everybody chill out and come down from the speedy ecstasy nice and easy. Eventually, everybody crashed. We were waking up when Kyle got home, and Kelly came around with waters and the biggest bottle of Advil I'd ever seen. Kyle told us that the girl who had passed out was a regular at that warehouse party every month. He knows some of her friends and is going to see if he can find out some details about what happened to her.

When we got home, Mom wanted to know all the details. We'd told her we were spending the night at Kelly's house after we went to an eighteen-and-under club with Reid, Carson, and Jess. Sometimes I think my mom just wants to believe what we're telling her so that she can live vicariously through our teenage lives. She didn't really get to do that much fun stuff when she was a kid. Her dad was sort of a mean drunk, and he ran off when she was in eighth grade, so the whole time she was in high school she had to work at a department store to help her mom make ends meet.

I thought Ashley would be done with her little drug experimentation phase, but she surprised me. She came into my room and told me that she had a really fun time this weekend. You could've knocked me over with a feather. And the thing is, I really think she meant it. It was weird. She gave me a big hug and called me "sis"—as if that were a totally normal thing or something she'd always called me.

THANK GOD tomorrow is Memorial Day. Dad and Mom are leaving me alone because I told them I have like a zillion tests this week for finals. Our last day of classes is on Friday, then graduation is on Saturday, but before then I have three papers due—two in AP English, and one in history. I have ZERO idea how all of this is going to get done, but I just have to plow through, starting NOW. I have to get the papers done before Dad makes us all come eat ribs. It's like his Memorial Day requirement: Everybody has to eat ribs. At least my parents are having friends over so I can just go down, eat a rib, then plead HOMEWORK and come back up here to finish studying.

Tuesday, May 27

This morning when we got to school, Ashley asked Jess first thing if Kelly was going to be able to get any "party favors" for the graduation party this weekend, and Jess winked at her and said she was sure that Kyle and Kelly would be able to figure something out. I figured that Ashley might have decided she was done experimenting, but apparently she had fun even though we witnessed that poor girl collapse on the dance floor.

At lunch Pete and Brandon stopped by where the rest of us were sitting. Carson got really tense, and sort of snapped at them. He told them to just keep walking. Brandon sneered and asked who died and made him the sheriff. Carson jumped up so fast his chair fell backward. Pete pulled Brandon away, but before he did, Carson said in a really quiet voice that the two of them had better back off. I get that Carson is upset about Brandon kissing me, but I didn't realize he has such a short fuse. I guess I thought he was a little more progressive than that. I mean, it's not like we've had a talk about us being boyfriend and girlfriend. It's not that I want to date anyone else—I don't. I just don't want him to think of me like I'm his property or something. At the same time, I don't want to make him think that I'm into Brandon or Pete or something.

This all feels difficult today—like nobody understands each

other, and things are getting all weird and mixed up. Or maybe it's just me. I wish I could cut the rest of my classes today, but after this study hall I have history and then after school we have to freaking march around the football field. Damn this Thanksgiving Day Parade. The last thing I want to do right now is walk in circles holding my clarinet.

After Pete and Brandon left the lunch table, Kelly called Jess. Kyle had just sent her a link to a news story about that girl who passed out at the club on Saturday. Apparently she took a couple tabs of ecstasy and a whole bunch of GHB—this party drug that you mix in a bottle and drink like Kool-Aid. I guess it makes you feel really drunk. At least that's what Reid said. He's done it a couple times before, but he says it's dangerous and you're not supposed to mix it with anything else—especially alcohol or other drugs. That girl is in critical condition in the hospital still.

I hope she'll be okay.

Wednesday, May 28

Jess and Kelly came over after dinner tonight, and Ashley and I went with them to go get some frozen yogurt at a self-serve place. While Kelly and I were sprinkling crushed-up Oreos on top of our chocolate/vanilla swirls, her phone buzzed. Once we got to a table out on the patio, Kelly checked the text message and she got this big grin on her face. She held the phone up to Jess, who yelled, HELLS YEAH! at the top of her lungs, startling everyone in about a three-mile radius.

The text was from Kyle. He'd scored some molly for this weekend. Ashley got all excited about it and texted Reid. About thirty seconds later, I had a text from Carson, confirming that Reid had told him. News travels fast.

The bummer about all of this is that Kelly can't go. The school doesn't allow students from other schools to come to the graduation party due to "issues of liability." You have to actually have a valid student ID to set foot in the place, and they usually have a police officer standing guard while the parent volunteers check everyone's name off a list just in case there's any issue. I'm not sure why kids from other schools can come to prom but not this party. I think it's because this party was all about keeping the "children" safe. I can just hear the school board meeting where irate mothers stood up and wailed, "Won't someone PLEASE think of the CHILDREN?" How is not allowing kids from other schools to come going to help? And what about, oh, I dunno, the night AFTER graduation? And all the nights after that when kids do dumb shit to celebrate getting out of high school?

Whatever.

Jess is planning to sneak Kelly in after we get inside. I'm sure THAT won't go horribly wrong. . . .

Jeez. What is wrong with me? I wish I were more excited about this. I video chatted with Carson after we got home from the yogurt place and we decided that we'd just drop and then go hang out with each other in the big beanbag pit in the band room. That way we won't have to deal with Jess and her crazy plan to sneak Kelly in through the fire escape—or however she's going to do it.

Carson is so cute. I could stare at his face on the screen for hours.

Saturday, May 31

So, we all went to graduation this morning. Reid and Carson got their diplomas, then both of their moms threw an "open house" party this afternoon. We went to Reid's first, and then Carson's. Met their grandparents and had food and cake and my mother almost embarrassed me to death in both places. Carson was smirking at me the whole time because he knows my mom drives me crazy. At one point he grabbed my hand and led me through the crowd in his backyard to his room, where he closed the door so we could make out for a little while. When we got back to the party, my mom was in the kitchen with his mom having a glass of wine, and she looked up and said, Well, there you two are!

She said this really loudly, as if to alert the entire neighborhood that we'd been making out somewhere. Carson walked me to the car when we left and said that he'd see me tonight. When we got back home, Jess and Kelly came over. Ashley came into my room and Kelly pulled out the bag of molly she'd scored from Kyle. Jess got increasingly excited about the party tonight while Ash looked completely terrified. She wanted to know how we were going to "do" it, and let it be known that there was no way she was going to snort anything up her nose. She asked if she could just put it in a drink or something, and Kelly warned her that this was a BAD idea. She explained that it tastes TERRIBLE and that it would ruin any liquid, and that she should "balloon it."

Ashley just blinked at her, and Kelly decided we should just go ahead and divvy it all up ahead of time. She got a mirror and showed Jess how to split up the doses evenly. Then she got some toilet paper and tore one square in half, dropped a little mound of powder into it, and twisted it up into a tiny pouch. Kelly did this for each dose, and then very carefully put them into the plastic bag and explained to Jess that it was extremely important that she keep the baggie tightly wrapped up so the little wads of molly didn't come undone and spill out all over the place. Jess said this was no problem and carefully put the baggie into her bra. Her rack is huge. It's not going to move at all wedged in there.

Carson and Reid are meeting us here, and then Kelly and Jess have their plan all worked out for when we get into the party tonight. I feel all nervous about this, but I can't really tell if I'm worried about getting caught or just excited about doing molly. It's weird, but I think there's not a lot of difference between feeling keyed up about having fun and terrified about getting caught having fun.

Carson just texted me:

We're on our way!

Sunday, June 1

I cannot believe how screwed I am. Note to self: If you have a feeling like it's a bad idea, PAY ATTENTION. I don't even know where to start. . . .

I guess at the beginning of the whole ridiculous evening and the party itself. The graduation bash is always a theme party. This year it was a Knights of the Round Table theme—King Arthur and Lancelot and Guinevere. The school booster club decorated the gym and the hallways to look like a medieval castle, but with lots of balloons. When we walked into the gym, there was a huge castle facade built across the front of the room with a drawbridge that let you walk across a moat, which was this big tank of water with fountains in it. It was actually really elaborate, and it must've taken a small army of people to pull off. I know a bunch of alumni who were back from college helped build it. Reid's dad is a contractor, and he headed up all the construction with his big crew.

Not that Reid could've been bothered to care about it at all. The moment we arrived he started badgering Jess to hand out the molly. Jess told him to cool his jets. We needed to let the place fill up a little and get the party started so it wasn't so obvious that there was a group of kids rolling.

We all went to get punch and explored. There were areas set up with board games, and another room with a bunch of carnival games like Skee-Ball and Whac-A-Mole. There was a big candy shop where you could raise your blood sugar by one billion points, which apparently half the kids had already done, because when the band started playing there was this mad rush to the middle of the dance floor in the gym.

The band was just okay. They sang covers of oldies and classic rock and a few more recent pop songs, but it was sort of like a bar mitzvah band, or one of those bands that sing Journey songs at wedding receptions. Still, Carson thought they were hilarious and he dragged me out onto the dance floor. Jess followed us and we all did these ridiculous dances. At one point, Jess was pretending to break-dance, and a circle formed around her as she did dance moves that were so funny, I was gasping for breath I was laughing so hard. Then Reid and Carson started dancing "back up" for her, and the whole thing looked like a *Saturday Night Live* sketch.

When the band took a break, the DJ the school had hired was all set up, and he started spinning some really cool mashups that were fun to dance to, but Reid was back to badgering Jess about the molly. Jess had been glued to her phone the whole night, and said that it was almost time. She was texting with Kelly about their planned rendezvous near the band room. There was a storage room we used for old timpani and music stands, the chairs the orchestra used, and lots of other stuff. It was a big room and had two doors that only opened from the inside out to the back parking lot. They were meant for loading and unloading equipment when we went to competitions. Tonight, Jess was planning to use the room for sneaking Kelly into the party.

The gym was packed at this point, and Jess took Ashley into the bathroom first. When they came back out, Ashley had this grin on her face, and danced up to us like she had done something spectacular. Reid told Jess and me to hurry—he was itching to roll like nobody I'd ever seen. Carson leaned down and gave me a kiss, then told Reid to cool his jets.

In the bathroom, Jess locked us into a stall, then fished the little baggie carefully out of her bra. She handed one little wad of molly to me and I popped it into my mouth as far back on my tongue as I could get it. I took a big gulp of water and felt the little bump sail down my throat. I took another swig just be sure. Jess was holding two bumps in her hand and she carefully rolled up the remaining two in the baggie and gave it to me. She told me to hold on to it for a second, then she popped one of the hits in her hand into her mouth, washed it down with some water, and grinned at me. She told me it was time to go get Kelly.

When we walked out of the bathroom, Carson and Reid were waiting for us in the hallway. Reid was dancing back and forth like a little kid who had to pee. Ashley was getting a drink at the water fountain, and as Carson leaned down to kiss me, I slipped the rolled-up baggie into the back pocket of his jeans. Dang, that boy has a hot butt. Carson winked at me, then headed into the boys' bathroom with Reid. I told him I'd meet him back in the gym in a second. Jess grabbed Ashley's hand and announced that she was coming with us, then we headed down the hall toward the music wing.

Kelly was waiting for us outside. As soon as Jess pushed open the door, Kelly slipped in and threw her arms around Jess's neck. They kissed for what seemed like a very long time, until Ashley told them to get a room. Then Kelly hopped onto a nearby rehearsal chair and threw both arms around Ashley, jumping onto her back like Ash was going to give her a piggyback ride. They both collapsed onto a pile of old band uniforms giggling, and Jess held out her hand to Kelly. Kelly tossed back the hit and chased it with a drink from my water bottle.

We all walked back toward the gym, passing through the band room, which was arranged with beanbag chairs. Not many people were in here yet. I knew that wouldn't change until people got tired of dancing, but it made me want to hurry up and go back with Carson. Suddenly I couldn't wait to see him again, and I realized I was starting to feel the molly already, even though it had only been about fifteen minutes since I dropped. Ashley's face seemed a little flushed and she kept oohing and aahing as we passed through the Mylar streamers that decorated the hallways. As we crossed the drawbridge over the moat at the front of the gym, Ashley stretched out her hands toward the fountain on the right and said it was SOOOOO BEAUTIFUUUUL.

Kelly and Jess and I all started laughing, and Jess said, Yep. Guess it's working.

All I could think about was grabbing Carson's butt again and getting him back to the biggest beanbag chair in the corner of the band room. Jess danced up to the boys, who were in the middle of the gym. When Reid turned around, he sniffed really loudly and Jess narrowed her eyes. Turns out the guys opened up their little wads of molly and snorted them off the toilet paper dispenser in the bathroom. Carson told me he was already feeling it in a major way, but it was dripping down the back of his throat and tasted like crap.

We went over and got some punch. Carson and Reid both gulped down a couple of glasses and then we all took bottles of water. About that time, the DJ started spinning this remix of an old-school Lady Gaga track and we all turned and ran back to the middle of the dance floor. Ashley let out a big WHOOOOOOOOOOOO! and started dancing in a circle with her arms above her head. Seeing her so loud and crazy made me wonder again about how smart it was to drop molly at a school party, but something about the music was just taking over my body.

There were tiny twinkle lights strung back and forth over the gym and they were suddenly dancing as hard as I was. The music pulsed through me, and I felt Carson's hand pull me in closer. We were all sandwiched together, our bodies pressed tight in the crush of people dancing. Reid and Ashley were whooping together now, and I thought about how molly affects everyone a little differently. Jess and Kelly get all quiet and giggly. They tell secrets and whisper to each other. Carson and I seem to become so close that we don't even need words to communicate. It was right as I was thinking this that Carson took my hand and led me past Ashley, who was making WOOT WOOT noises and dirty dancing with Reid. I could tell that everything was too intense for Carson, and that he was taking me to the band room to find a quiet corner.

I wondered if I should stay and keep an eye on Ashley, but it was hard to worry about my sister when I felt so good. I know now, looking back, that was the molly doing its work. I didn't have a care in the world. The drug had taken me over. The only thing I could focus on was this moment, with Carson; how excited and happy I was to be winding through the streamers and lights and bodies and music, down one hall and up another, stopping here and there to stare into his eyes, and smile. He sniffed every now and then, and from time to time, he'd stop and gently kiss me.

There were board games set up in the chemistry room, and

we briefly stood near a group of guys from the track team who were involved in a Hungry Hungry Hippos tournament. The clattering of the plastic hippo heads as they gobbled marbles grew louder and louder, along with the shouts of the guys working the tiny levers. Finally, with a loud roar of yells and cheers, the entire game board flipped into the air from their wild enthusiasm, sending marbles flying in all directions.

Carson and I laughed and ran from the doorway of the room, racing around corners and past parents telling us to slow down and be careful. Finally we collapsed onto a beanbag in the band room and lay there panting and staring up at the ceiling tiles. The designs in the soundproof fiberglass tiles seemed to wiggle in a strange and hilarious routine, and I knew from Carson's soft "Wow" that he was seeing it too. We were the only people in the band room, which I didn't really think about until Mr. Peterson came into the room. The sound of his loafers against the tile floor in the hallway echoed strangely in my ears, like a *whoosh-splahsh!* It sounded like he was running through water. I turned my head and saw him come into the room, and he jumped a little—like he was surprised to see anyone here at all.

He said my name, and told Carson "congrats." He asked us if we were having a good time. I just smiled at him. I couldn't have talked right then even if I'd wanted to. Luckily, Carson seemed pretty with it. He sat up next to me on the beanbag and said, Hey, Mr. P. Thanks! Then Carson told him that we were taking a break from dancing. Then a big group of sophomore girls who I recognized from the volleyball team came in, and one of them did a somersault onto a beanbag chair. Mr. Peterson told her not to do that again because he didn't want to have to take her to the emergency room.

Just as Carson kissed me again, Reid and Ashley showed up. Ashley came running over and plopped onto the beanbag next to mine. Reid took the beanbag on the other side, and Ashley spotted Mr. Peterson and popped back up, running over to where he was talking to the volleyball girls. I heard her say, Mr. Peterson! like he was her long-lost friend, and then start talking about how much she had loved being in band as a freshman. Ashley gave up playing the flute this year. Mr. Peterson was saying something back to her, but I don't really remember what it was because Reid and Carson and I were all staring at the ceiling tiles again, and Reid (who was sweaty as hell from dancing) kept saying, Far OUT. I noticed he was chewing some gum like it was his job and asked him where he got it. He pulled a pack out of his pocket and said that Kelly had given it to him to share. As Carson and I were each taking a piece, Carson said he was thirsty and I asked him to bring me back some water or some punch or something. He kissed me, and as I watched him walk toward the door, I felt someone kneel down on the floor next to my beanbag. I turned to see Mr. Peterson.

There was a look on his face that I can't quite explain. It was as if he were doing a math problem that had a complicated solution, and he was just about to solve it. I sat up on the beanbag and he smiled at me and said, I don't want to alarm you, but I think your sister might be high. Do you have your parents' phone number handy so that I can call them and have them come pick Ashley up?

Of course, right then Reid started giggling like a maniac. He hadn't heard any of this conversation. He was just tripping out on the beanbag, running his hands over the cool, smushy vinyl and pointing up at the patterns in the ceiling tiles. I wanted to tell him to shut the hell up. I wanted to be able to sit up and fish my phone out of my pocket, to hand it to Mr. Peterson and say I was so sorry about Ashley, and that I would call my parents to have them come get her right away.

Instead, I just stared into Mr. Peterson's eyes. I remember thinking, I wonder if anyone loves Mr. Peterson the way that I love Carson? It felt like the deepest, most amazing thing I'd ever considered. It brought a thrilling wave of emotion crashing over me, and suddenly every inch of me was covered in goose bumps. I remember thinking that I could be that person. I could love Mr. Peterson the way that Carson loved me.

And that's when I leaned up and kissed Mr. Peterson on the tip of his nose.

Yep.

I kissed the tip of his nose.

It seemed like it would fix everything. I was certain of it. Nothing would make more sense, or make him feel better, or make me feel more alive. It just seemed like the perfect thing to do.

Needless to say, I was wrong.

Mr. Peterson figured out that I was on something too, and it was pretty clear that Reid was high as a freaking kite. He was still giggling at the ceiling tiles when my dad showed up in the doorway of the band room, and in front of the entire school, Ashley and I got led out of the party by our elbows. Carson had seen what was going down when he came back to the room with our drinks and had gone to warn Jess and Kelly. They immediately split, and Kelly called Kyle, who came and picked them up on the corner by the football field.

Mr. Peterson had his hands full with Reid until Reid's mom showed up, but Reid had already graduated, so he got off easy.

There's nothing they can really do to him. Me and Ashley on the other hand? We're screwed. We don't know exactly what the punishment will be yet, but suffice it to say that we're in deep shit.

Oh, and just for the record, molly doesn't make your parents yelling at you any more fun. It's awful. I couldn't figure out what was going on, and the less I paid attention to my mom, the angrier she got.

I've been awake for a couple hours now, but I'm dreading going downstairs to the kitchen. I can only imagine what's waiting for me there.

Later . . .

Just got done with dinner. It may have been the worst meal of my entire life. Dad is so upset that he's not even yelling, he's just got this look on his face like he doesn't even know who we are anymore. Of course, Mom is yelling enough for both of them. She talked the entire time we were at the table about how foolish we are. "Foolish." Again and again she said that word. Ashley was a moron and kept trying to argue with her. She kept trying to convince Mom that molly isn't that dangerous. Of course, Mom has been online all day and is now armed with "facts" about drug use.

It's weird because she barely even talked to me. It's almost like she expects me to do something this "foolish" but not Ashley. Not her perfect, straight-A student. Ashley was going to run for student council next fall, but now Mom has made it clear that this is off the table. And we don't even know what the school is going to do. Mr. Peterson told them that he is going to talk with Principal Andrews and that she is going to make the final call.

Ashley was stupid for fighting back. At least I knew better than to flap my mouth. Ashley was trying to tell Mom that she did know where the drugs came from, that they were "tested" to make sure they were clean. It would've been hilarious to watch them go at it if it weren't so crazy. Of course, Ash has it in her head that she can fix this somehow, but she's trying not to rat out Kelly. If she tells Mom that Kelly was involved, Mom will never let us hang out with Kelly, and maybe Jess, ever again.

But Ash has never been in trouble before so she doesn't get it. She doesn't understand that Mom is not going to let us out of her sight for the next month, at least. We're both grounded and Mom and Dad won't even say for how long, only that we can't go anywhere for a long time.

I just sat there and pretended to eat. I'm not really hungry. I'm just so freaking glad that Carson left to get us water when he did. Mom kept asking Ashley where she got the drugs, and eventually decided that Reid gave them to us. Ashley was trying to defend Reid, and Mom said, Well, you can stop sticking up for him. You're never going out with him again.

Ashley dissolved into tears and stomped away from the table when she heard this. Once she was gone, Mom stormed off too, leaving me and my dad sitting in this uncomfortable silence at the dinner table, staring at our plates, the ceiling, out the window, anywhere really except at each other. I finally got up and started to clear the table. As I was taking plates and glasses to the sink, Dad said, Just don't.

I stopped and looked at him, and he was crying. Not like sobbing or anything, just had tears running down his cheeks. He told me just to go to my room, and it made my stomach turn. He's so disappointed with us—I think with me especially. He doesn't even want to be in the same room as me. I put the dishes I was holding in the sink and came back to my room.

Carson texted me to check in, and I told him I was grounded for the foreseeable future. He asked what that meant, and I said that I wasn't sure, only that I wouldn't be able to see him for a while probably. He texted back that he was sorry about everything, and to keep him posted. I can't believe he said he was sorry. For what? This is really all my fault. I knew that we shouldn't try to roll at the graduation party. I should have been the one to put my foot down, but I just couldn't say no to feeling the way that molly makes me feel. Actually, it's not that I couldn't, I just didn't want to.

Jesus. What a way to start the summer.

Thursday, June 5

Principal Andrews called Mom today. She decided that Ashley and I are suspended from the first day of school next year. Also, she and Mr. Peterson talked, and I can't go to the Thanksgiving Day Parade with the marching band. For someone who has always thought of band as something that only nerds do, Mom sure was livid about the whole thing. When she told me, I started crying, but she said I should dry my tears because I brought all of this on myself.

I ran to my room crying, and Ashley followed me in here and slammed the door. She blamed me for "getting her involved in all of this." As if I'm the one who begged her to do molly with us. I started to argue with her, to tell her that she was the one who insisted that we roll at the graduation party because Reid was so into it, and she went ballistic. She kept yelling about how her permanent record was "tarnished" now. She's such a little bitch. I didn't hold her and shove molly down her throat. I didn't want her to do it at all. I wanted to hang out with my friends and do my own thing, but she was the one who had to get involved.

Carson and Jess have been texting me like crazy for updates. Jess keeps asking if she can come over. I keep telling her no. She has it in her head that she can try to smooth things over with my mom, and I keep telling her that right now Mom is on the warpath, so she should steer clear if she ever wants to see me again.

I guess this is the part of molly that is the opposite of "pure bliss."

But you know something? If I have the chance to do it again, I will. I don't care how bad this feels right now. Nothing feels as good as doing molly.

Saturday, June 14

It has been thirteen days since I left the house without my mother or father. It's like I'm six years old again. I guess I never really think about how much I come and go as I please. My parents are generally pretty cool about stuff like curfews and letting me go places with my friends, but the past two weeks I haven't even asked. I know better.

Dad has stopped staring at me like I'm a stranger, and gradually Mom has even lightened up a little bit. Ashley, on the other hand, glares at me like I'm the source of every problem in the whole world, and hasn't spoken to me except to ask me to pass food when we are sitting down at dinner. Whatever. She can blame everybody in the world for this, but she was the one who had to go up and talk to Mr. Peterson. If she hadn't gushed all over him like a crazy person, he wouldn't have come to find me. And if he hadn't come to find me, I wouldn't have kissed him on the nose.

Did that really happen?

Reading that sentence just made me laugh for the first time in almost two weeks.

Last night we had Family Movie Night just like it was any other Friday. Only instead of watching a movie, Dad had us all watch this episode of a show called *Drugs, Inc.* on National Geographic. It was about molly and the Seattle rave scene. In the episode, all these people are doing molly and talking about it. Of course, they highlight all the "terrible" ways in which molly is dangerous—how it raises your body temperature and puts you at risk of dehydration and blah, blah, blah. Guess what? It made me want to roll. It also made me want to try snorting molly next time. They talked about how the high was faster and more direct. I remembered that it certainly seemed to be that way for Carson and Reid.

Carson texted me today and asked what I was doing tonight—

like he didn't know. We've been playing this game where he texts me and asks what I'm up to, and I make up ridiculous replies like:

Getting a tattoo of an elephant on my left shoulder.

Having tea with Kate Middleton and trying on her hats.

Packing for a trip to Paris with Emma Stone.

But today I wasn't in the mood so I just texted him that I was LOSING MY MIND. He texted back a picture of him, Jess, and Kelly with the words:

We're coming to spring you from prison. Be ready at 11. He spins at 12AM!

This awesome DJ that Kyle turned us all on to is playing a show tonight. The DJ is called Whip5mart and he's supposedly spinning at this underground party Kyle knows about. It's sort of a traveling rave, and this month it's being held in an abandoned swimming pool in a part of town I am not allowed to go to by myself. I mean, right now I'm not allowed to go anywhere by myself, but I mean under normal circumstances.

But I was serious about losing my mind. I have to get out of here. Mom and Dad are usually in bed by ten thirty on Saturdays, and Ashley has been locking herself in her room as soon as dinner is over. She's been crying a lot because last time Reid called, Mom told him that he could stop calling because Ashley isn't allowed to date him anymore.

So, he stopped calling.

If you ask me, Reid is being exactly the douche that I thought he was to begin with. If your girlfriend's parents tell you not to see her anymore and you really like her, do you let that stop you? I asked Carson the same thing once about the girl he was supposed to bring to prom. He admitted that he just wasn't that into her. He felt like her parents did him a favor because he was going to break up with her after prom.

Anyway, I said I'd be ready at midnight. I told him to park at the end of the block. I'll just go out the back door in the garage and let myself out onto the sidewalk from the side gate in the backyard. As long as I'm home by five a.m. I should be able to sneak back in, and no one will even know I was gone.

Sunday, June 15

I am so scared. I'm exhausted, but I can't sleep. It's almost five a.m. I took a shower after I got home, but even the hot water washing away all the sweat and smoke wouldn't wash away this feeling in my chest. I keep checking my phone to see if Carson or Kelly has texted me any updates on Jess, but there's nothing.

I'm not high anymore, but I still feel a little spaced out. It's one of the reasons I wanted to try to write all of this down. I want it to make sense and it doesn't yet in my head. Maybe I can put the words down on paper and the whole story will come together, but all I can see in my head is Jess on that stretcher. I guess I should start at the beginning.

Jess drove.

She stopped to pick up Kelly and Carson, then they came to my place and parked at the end of the block like I'd told them to. Mom and Dad had gone to bed around ten thirty, and Ashley had been in her room with the door closed all night, just like I'd guessed.

Of course, I hit every single squeaky stair and floorboard on my way through the house to the garage, and the hinges on that door squealed like a cat being run over by an eighteen wheeler. I stood still, heart racing, listening for any sound from my parents' bedroom. Then I stepped into the garage and swung the door closed as quickly as possible without slamming it. I was panting as I slipped out the back door of the garage and ran across the damp grass of the backyard to the side gate, where I let myself out onto the sidewalk.

I felt giddy once I got to the street. The moon was remarkably bright, and I could see Jess's car at the end of the block. I started laughing as the back door of the car swung open and I jumped in next to Carson, who immediately wrapped both arms around me and kissed me for a long time as Jess pulled away from the curb, shrieking and hooting with Kelly.

I was lost in Carson's kiss. He smelled like warm brown sugar and his peppery cologne, and underneath his peppermint gum there was just the hint of a cigarette—but not in a gross ashtray sort of way; it was smoky in a sexy, bad-boy sort of way. When we came up for air, I filled everybody in on my incarceration. Jess agreed that it sounded pretty terrible and Kelly couldn't believe that I had kissed Mr. Peterson on the nose. She kept giggling about it, then getting control of herself, then collapsing into laughter again in the front seat. Carson said that it was "epic" and kept apologizing for taking off with Jess and Kelly. I assured him that there was nothing he could've done, and if he'd been there he'd have just gotten busted, too.

When we got to the park where the old abandoned swimming

pool was, there were cars parked all up and down the road leading up to the entrance. Carson said it looked like we'd have to walk, but Jess said SCREW THAT and drove right up to the fence around the pool. We could see the lights flashing from the scaffolding rigged around the pool, and there was a line of people at the door to the old locker-room entrance. Jess drove around to the opposite side of the pool from where the line was, pulled over the curb between a couple of trees, and parked in the grass next to some picnic tables. We all started laughing and Carson just shook his head and told Jess she was off the hook.

It was really dark in the car. The trees towering over us blocked out most of the light from the moon and the flashing lights over the empty pool. Carson was texting Reid, who was apparently just meeting us there. He was walking all the way up from where he'd parked on the street and he finally found Jess's car. He tapped on Carson's window and then Carson slid over to my side of the backseat and opened the door. Reid got into the car and a girl climbed in after him. It was pretty cramped in the backseat with all four of us—especially since Carson is so tall. He scooted under me, and I sort of wedged myself sideways on his lap.

The girl with Reid was named Sara and was one of Derrick's

sisters who had just gotten home from her freshman year of college. When Reid saw me there he looked a little sheepish and said, Hey. He introduced me to Sara and then he just laughed and said, Well . . . this is really freaking weird. But it wasn't a mean laugh or an asshole laugh, it was more like a moment that we were sharing. It wasn't a laugh that was meant to keep me out. It was a laugh that let me in.

Kelly handed out capsules of molly to each of us, and I took mine from her and just shrugged at Reid. I said, Who doesn't want to feel this good? My sister, that's who. Then I smiled, popped the capsule into my mouth, and swallowed. Reid smiled back at me as Kelly announced that she had two hits for each of us and that this stuff was the purest that Kyle had ever seen. We all slipped her some cash for the party favors. She said that we could wait to do the second hits until we were in the party, but Jess said she wanted to do hers now.

I got a little nervous, but everybody agreed. Jess said she wanted to snort hers and Reid and Carson said they did too. Kelly and Sara didn't want to taste it in the back of their mouths all night, so they just swallowed theirs, but I let Carson dump out my second capsule. The powder was tiny, light brown crystals. He crunched it up on a little case that Kelly had in her purse. It was the size of a large makeup compact, but instead of a mirror inside, it folded out into a little metal tray. Carson used his ATM card to crunch up the crystals a little smaller and then tapped the powder into a line. There was a little straw in the case and he held it toward me. I put one end of the straw into my nose and sniffed up the line of powder, just like he had.

YEOWCH. It totally burns to snort powder into your nose. And then the taste that flooded down the back of my throat and into my mouth? It was terrible. It was like I was chewing on a latex glove. But damn, by the time we got to the door of the old locker rooms, I was already dancing. Carson was walking behind me, his hand on my hips, his fingers hooked in my belt loops. He was laughing and directing me through the old tile rooms toward the door that led out to the pool. We heard a big cheer as we stepped out onto the concrete pool deck, and saw that Whip5mart had just stepped behind the big deck of equipment between two diving boards. The blue slope of concrete was covered with a mass of bodies, and I couldn't wait to get down into it. The music had hit my feet and it was a totally physical experience. All I wanted to do was dance.

The molly washed over me in waves unlike anything I'd ever felt before. Carson and I were silent as we danced, and I could almost feel the beats hitting my skin like raindrops. Reid and Sara danced behind Carson, and Jess and Kelly were to our right. The six of us could barely talk to each other. Every once in a while, Carson would pull me in and kiss me. He and Reid had peeled off their shirts a long time ago—was it hours? I didn't know how long we'd been dancing. His hair was wet with sweat and seemed to be glowing purple under the lights. I knew it was just the drug playing tricks on my eyes, but it was a beautiful trick.

As Whip5mart shifted into a quieter, down-tempo track, Carson threw his head back and whooped. Reid laughed and told Jess and Kelly that this molly was the SHIT. Sara said she needed some gum 'cause she was gurning really badly. Kelly handed her a couple sticks out of her hip pocket and I realized Sara was talking about the tension in her jaw. I felt it too, and Carson rescued me with some gum of his own. He grabbed my hand and we followed Reid and Sara, who were headed to get some water at the old pool snack bar. I yelled for Jess to come too, and I'll never forget the look on her face. There was sweat pouring down her cheeks from dancing, but she had this huge grin and was staring up into the lights as she and Kelly danced like they were on a different plane of existence.

After we waded through the lines, Carson slapped down a twenty and we all had waters. Then he led us through a hole in the chain-link fence to the picnic tables near where we'd parked.

We all sat down on one of the tables and he and Reid passed around a pack of cigarettes. I hate the smell of smoke, and I've only smoked a cigarette a couple times, but the gum, the water, and the waves of feeling that were pouring over me made me think that a smoke would be the PERFECT thing. Carson looked surprised when I took a cigarette, but then he leaned toward me with his lighter and sparked it to life.

The first inhale made me cough a little, but then the buzz of the nicotine hit me and made the lights from the pool flash in my eyes like a starburst. I started giggling as I blew out my second drag of smoke, and Carson and I talked with Reid and Sara about how amazing this all was. The pool seemed to be alive—like it was a giant creature with all these limbs, flailing and bouncing in time to the music. We all agreed that we were rolling like crazy. Reid said that the second hit had sent him over the moon, and Sara and I agreed.

After we finished our cigarettes and talked for a little while longer, we slipped back through the fence. It was a lot cooler on the deck around the pool than it was being down in the crush of bodies, so we started dancing by an abandoned lifeguard stand where this girl in a bikini was standing twirling glow sticks. The lights from the party were dancing off Carson's chest and abs, and I hooked a finger into the waistband of his jeans next to where he'd hung his T-shirt and pulled him close to me. I think he is the most handsome creature I've ever laid eyes on. Even with all the fear in my stomach right now, and feeling dazed while I write this all down, the memory of his smile makes me get goose bumps down my spine and makes my breath a little short. I want him here right now to touch me, to kiss me, to run his hands across my chest and down my stomach. I want to feel his fingers pulling off my underwear and tugging me toward him.

Jeez. I'm blushing while I write this, but I don't care. That's how I felt dancing next to Carson at the pool—like everything was plugged into a socket and I wanted him plugged into me. There was fire in my legs and ice down my arms. I reached up to throw my arms around his neck, and as I did, I saw him look over my shoulder. The pupils of his eyes were like big black olives—you could barely see any of the color of his irises. As I looked into his eyes I saw lights flashing from behind us, and saw chasers of red and blue squiggles, but there was something else, too: a sound wailing over the music.

I whirled around and Carson started pushing through the crowd. There was an ambulance and it was so overwhelming—the visuals and the sounds and the people—I wouldn't have been able to keep up with Carson if he hadn't reached back and grabbed my hand. He was tall enough to see over everybody else and glimpse what was happening at the bottom of the pool before I did. As we got to the edge I saw three paramedics. One was holding a light and an IV bag up in the air. The other two were bent over a rolling stretcher that they had carried into the pool. There was a circle of people around them, clearing space as the rest of the party danced, completely unaware that there was something happening in the other end of the pool.

My eyes followed the tube from the IV bag into the arm of the person on the stretcher. Two medics jerked upward on the rails of the stretcher as they lifted it onto the edge of the pool and climbed out. The legs and wheels underneath the gurney unfolded, and they started rolling the patient past us toward the ambulance.

As they passed, I saw that the person on the stretcher was Jess. I slipped my hand out of Carson's and ran as fast as I could. I was within a couple feet of the stretcher when someone stepped into my path, and as I tried to push past them, I felt two arms wrap around me and heard my name.

I looked down, blinking, and saw that it was Kelly. Carson, Reid, and Sara caught up with me, and we were all shouting questions at Kelly at the same time. She waved us all over to the hole in the chain link and we congregated by the picnic tables.

Kelly explained that Jess hadn't had enough water to drink and was just dehydrated. I was crying and kept yelling JUST? She's JUST DEHYDRATED? Kelly kept trying to shush me, and that just pissed me off, but Carson finally wrapped both arms around me and walked me away from the group. We sat under a tree, and he explained to me that we had to let the paramedics take Jess to the hospital. That she'd be okay.

All of this was a blur to me at the time, but eventually, he handed me his cigarette and I took a few drags and calmed down. Kelly called her brother, Kyle, who called Jess's parents and told them she was headed to the hospital. Then he came to pick us up. It was still dark, but the sky was getting a shade lighter as we all piled into Kyle's white SUV. Kelly told him to take me home first, and we were all pretty quiet as we drove through the predawn streets. There was no traffic that early in the morning. Carson put his arm around me and whispered that he was sure Jess would be okay. I couldn't stop the tears from slipping quietly down my cheeks. It wasn't so much that I was sad as I was scared. Scared for Jess, and scared about what had just happened.

When Kyle pulled onto my street, I told him to stop where Jess had picked me up earlier, and after one more kiss from Carson, I slipped out of the car, walked up the street to the side gate, and let myself into the house. I didn't even care about getting caught anymore. I just wanted to get to my room so I could take a shower and be by myself. I tiptoed across the living room and when I got to my room I slipped out of my sweaty clothes and took a long, hot shower. I thought I'd want to go directly to bed, but I still must have some of the drugs in my system, because I just lay there, wide awake. That's when I decided to get up and write it all down.

I guess there's nothing left to do now but sleep and maybe pray. Pray that Jess will be okay.

Later...

ASHLEY IS A PAIN IN MY ASS.

She just left my room. I had just crawled back into bed when the door opened and Ashley came in and turned on the light. I sat up and looked at her—not quite understanding what was happening. She glared at me and said, I know what's going on.

My mind was racing because I didn't know what exactly she was referring to. Did she know that I'd snuck out? Did she somehow know about Jess? I wasn't in the dark long. She was whispering at me—a loud, angry whisper. She started off by telling me that I wasn't fooling anyone, especially HER. She told me that she'd gone to get some water last night and she saw me as I was crossing the backyard to let myself out the side gate.

She said she knew I was going out to do more molly and if I didn't promise to stop rolling she was going to tell Mom and Dad that I'd snuck out. That threat, that ultimatum, made all the things I really hate about her come rolling over me. All of her popular-girl prettiness and how left out I'd always felt spun around in my chest and made me go blind with rage. I couldn't believe how angry I was. I told her to shut the hell up and that she didn't know what she was talking about, but she just stared at me with her ice queen eyes and said, Fine. Let's go tell Mom and Dad right now.

I was so pissed off that I stopped her the only way I knew how. I said, Reid was there, you know.

At the sound of his name, Ashley spun around and there was the faintest spark of hope in her eyes. As she opened her mouth to ask about him, I felt the rage in my chest bubble up through my lips. I told her that he was there with a new girl—a college girl. That Derrick's sister Sara was all over him. That they were dancing and kissing and feeling each other up in the middle of the music and lights and dancing. As I said the words, I saw her whole face crumple in on itself, but I couldn't stop. She was crying and telling me to stop, but I kept going. I told her how Reid had laughed about her with me. How he didn't care about her anymore, and maybe he'd never cared about her at all.

I told her that she was just jealous of me now. That all my life I'd been the nerdy older sister. The band geek who never got invited to anything. That now the tables had turned. I asked her how she liked being the girl who was stuck at home while I went out with my hot boyfriend. She couldn't even answer me. She just ran out of my room crying.

I was so angry after she left I was shaking. I can barely hold this pen. And you know something? I don't feel bad about saying those things. After all the years where I was like a freaking second-class citizen in this family, I don't give a shit if I hurt her feelings. She should know how it feels. Here's a taste of your own medicine, Ashley. Sucks, doesn't it?

Monday, June 16

I just got back from seeing Jess. Carson came over this morning after my dad went to work. He just showed up on the front porch and rang the doorbell. My mom was working in her office down the hall and I heard her pass my room to go and answer. I just figured it was the UPS man or something, but when she opened the door, I heard her say, Oh! Hi, Carson! in this sort of surprised, cheery voice.

Thank god I'd gotten up and taken a shower this morning

and put on some eyeliner. I was hoping to convince my mom to let me go to the library or the grocery store or SOMEWHERE today, so I had gotten dressed in halfway decent clothes already too. When I heard her say his name, I opened my door and stuck my head into the hallway, just as she called up the stairs for me to come down.

Carson was wearing nice jeans and a short-sleeved button-up plaid shirt. He looked very nice, and he was holding flowers. When I came into the entryway next to the front door, he smiled at me, and my mom told me, I wish I had a young man showing up on my doorstep with flowers. Then Carson did something that was truly remarkable. He said, Oh, these ARE for you, and held the bouquet out toward my mom. Before I knew what was happening, my mom was standing there holding a fistful of pink gerbera daisies and blinking at Carson like he was a heavenly apparition. He smiled at her and said, I was hoping you'd let me take her to pick out her own flowers.

If anyone besides Carson tried this stunt, it would've backfired miserably. If he'd tried it with any mother but my own, it probably wouldn't have worked. But Carson is just that kind of guy—so charming that it catches you off guard. And I think my mom has always secretly wanted to be Ashley—the pretty, popular one. Carson made her feel that way. Mom actually giggled, and then said she thought that might be okay, as long as we weren't gone long. Carson explained that Jess wasn't feeling well, and that he'd hoped he could drive me by her house for a visit to cheer her up.

Mom expressed all sorts of concern for Jess and asked me why I hadn't said anything about it. I've been texting Jess a lot since I saw her on that stretcher at the swimming pool—all day Sunday and off and on all day yesterday. I've been going out of my mind. She hasn't texted me back once. Not a single time. Which is sort of unheard of. It filled me with dread that something was really wrong with her. Carson and I had video chatted last night and he said that he'd gotten ahold of Kelly and she said that Jess was okay and at home now. This just made it seem even weirder that she wasn't texting me back.

I shrugged and told my mom that I knew Jess wasn't feeling well but didn't think she'd have let me go see her anyway, and then Mom acted like that was preposterous. She acted like I wasn't grounded—like she'd forgotten all about the graduation party incident two weeks ago—and made it seem like the most ridiculous thing in the world that I suggested she wouldn't have let me go. Then she made it sound like it was the most important thing in the world for me and Carson go cheer Jess up. She said to take our time and just be home before dinner.

Well, let's just say that you don't have to tell me twice. I wasn't about to question this. I grabbed my purse and keys. As I was walking out the door with Carson, I looked up and saw Ashley standing on the top stair, leaning against the wall. Her arms were folded, and she had a look on her face like she'd just sucked on a lemon. A chill shot down my spine, but I forced myself to smile, and then turned on my heel and left with Carson.

When we rolled up in front of Jess's house, Carson took off his seat belt, then pulled me toward him and started kissing me. He told me how much he missed me. I laughed and told him that I couldn't believe he just showed up at my front door. He smiled slyly and said, I thought your mom might be a pushover if I brought her flowers.

We got out of the car and rang the doorbell at Jess's house. It took her a really long time to come to the door, and when she opened it, she didn't seem to be feeling very well. She looked a little pale, but more than that, she wasn't smiling or her usual bubbly self. She frowned at us and looked kind of pained, like this was a big nuisance having to open the door. She said hi, and just stood there. I moved in to give her a hug, but she didn't hug me back, just kept her hand on the doorknob. I told her how happy I was that she was okay, and how when I saw her on that stretcher, I couldn't stop crying. I explained that I had tried to chase the medics but Kelly had stopped me.

Jess just looked at us. She didn't say anything, and the longer she stood there silently, the stranger I felt. Finally, I glanced at Carson and then back at Jess and asked her if we could come in. She shrugged and pushed the door all the way open, then turned around and headed into her living room. She curled up on the couch and stared at the television, which was on, but the sound was muted.

I asked if she was okay, and Jess told us that she was fine, just dehydrated. She said they'd kept her in the hospital until they'd given her a ton of fluids. Her mom showed up to get her and was really scared, but she said that her dad had just told her to stop doing drugs like some hippie party girl, and then left on another business trip. I was sitting on the couch next to Jess and when she said this I reached over and grabbed her hand. I told her again how happy I was that she was okay, and that next time we'd remember to make sure everybody drank plenty of water.

Jess sort of scoffed when I said this and pulled her hand away. She punched a button on the remote and the TV flickered off. Then she looked at me and asked if I was crazy. I frowned but didn't say anything. Jess was acting so weird. She looked at me and then Carson, and shook her head and ran a hand over her face and through her hair. She told me there wasn't going to be a "next time."

I frowned and I guess I looked a little shocked when I asked her if she was serious because she got angry—not yelling Ashley-style, but I could tell my question had annoyed her. She shot back a terse, Yes, REALLY! and then stared at me and Carson really hard. Her eyes were cold. She said she wasn't going to roll again because she couldn't trust her friends to look out for her.

When she said that, I felt like she had slapped me across the face. I looked at Carson and then back to Jess. I opened my mouth to argue, but Jess held up a hand and told me to give it a rest. I felt my eyes fill up with tears, but before I could say or do anything, Carson stood up and said, Okay, well, we just wanted to check on you and make sure you were okay.

Jess bitterly said she was fine like she was implying it was no thanks to us. And then Carson and I were standing on the sidewalk in front of her house. I was still reeling. I couldn't believe that my best friend in the whole world basically blamed me for her own stupid mistake. It wasn't MY fault that she didn't drink enough water. It wasn't MY fault that she was a heavy girl and probably needed more water than the rest of us because she was sweating so much more while she danced. I felt this terrible, gross anger in the pit of my stomach—different from what I felt when Ashley was in my room yesterday. This hurt worse. Ashley and I are sisters, so what if we don't have to like each other? We're family. But Jess? I've had her back for years. What did this mean for our friendship?

Carson opened the passenger door to his car and waited for me to get in, then he drove us to his house. His dad and mom were both at work, and we went out by the pool and sat down and put our feet in the water. He got us beers from the fridge and poured them into plastic glasses, leaving the glass bottles in the kitchen. He talked to me for a long time—actually he just listened. I ranted about how self-righteous Jess was being, and he said that she and Kelly were in a big fight about all of this too. Jess apparently blamed Kelly for calling her parents. Kelly had tried to explain that she couldn't have gone to the hospital with Jess and accomplished anything. They had to know.

After a while we went back inside, and one thing led to another. The beer had made me light-headed, and pretty soon Carson and I were both naked and he was kissing me between my legs. It felt so amazing that I just let him keep doing it until I felt a familiar buzz and hum course through my body—a feeling I'd only given myself before. Then I pulled him back up next to me on his bed and returned the favor. I could tell he wanted to be inside me, but I wasn't in the right head space for all that. Not that it was so different from what we had just done, but it felt like a big step for our relationship somehow. He said it was the best blow job he'd ever had in his life. I asked if he'd had a lot, and he didn't really answer, but I didn't really care. Carson isn't a bullshitter. That's one of the things that makes me feel comfortable with him. What you see is what you get.

As he drove me back home, I turned on some music, and he reached over and took my hand. We didn't say anything else until he parked in my driveway. He turned to me and said, We should hang out again tomorrow. I told him I was down with that if my mom was. He told me that he wanted to hang out with our friend molly tomorrow, and I know I got this big surprised look on my face.

Carson explained that he'd gotten Kyle's number the other night when he dropped us off after the Whip5mart concert fiasco and had scored some more molly yesterday. He'd always wanted to roll in the daytime, and his mom and dad would be at work all day tomorrow. I couldn't lie. It sounded like the best idea ever.

I don't care what Jess and Ashley say. I don't want to stop

rolling. I love doing molly. I love doing it with Carson. I'm excited about it just being him and me tomorrow.

Tuesday, June 17

Carson stayed for dinner just now, which was an experience and a half—especially after our day together. I hadn't intended to ask him in when he brought me home today, but my mom actually stepped out onto the front porch to wave at us as we pulled into the driveway, and insisted that Carson join us for dinner. Ashley didn't come out of her room until dinner was served, and she sat down and immediately started grilling Carson on what we did today until my mom said, Ashley, maybe you could pass me the spinach salad and stop grilling our guest like he's on *Law & Order*, which made me laugh with water in my mouth and it almost came out my nose.

He did a great job of carrying on a conversation with my mom and dad. Thank god. I was still coming down from our little day trip.

Carson stopped by this morning around ten with a small box of doughnuts and sweet-talked my mom into letting him "steal me" for the day to help him pick out a birthday present for his mother. This was not a complete lie. Carson's mom does have a birthday coming up next month, but he's already picked out the present. It's this clock at a store that sells furniture from the 1960s, and it looks like a starburst with little hands in the middle. Anyway, he and my mom immediately got into this conversation about the design from that time and tossed around the names of all these designers that Carson's mom loves.

By the time we'd all finished a cup of coffee and a doughnut, Mom was sold and told me to have a good time and be sure to be home for dinner. I started laughing as Carson pulled out of the driveway, and he smiled his sly little smile and asked what was so funny. I just said, Shouldn't it be harder than this? I told him that he has some sort of evil power over my mother, and he told me that he actually really likes my mom. I just stared at him like he was crazy. This is exactly what I was talking about: He doesn't mess around. He's not pretending. If he seems to really like somebody, it's not because he's putting on an act.

Today was one of the first days it was over eighty degrees, so it was a perfect day to hang out by the pool. We changed in his bedroom. That's another thing I like about him—he's not shy. Not that he should be. His body is off the hook from football and track. He's totally comfortable in his own skin. And something about him being so comfortable pulling off his T-shirt and then kicking out of his shorts made me totally comfortable too. Carson wasn't wearing any underwear under his gym shorts and he didn't act like a little boy and turn around to try to hide his front side from me. He picked up his shorts and folded them and put them on the bed, then walked over to his dresser and pulled out a pair of swim trunks. As he did, he glanced over at me and caught me full-on staring at him.

He paused for a second and smirked. Then, as he rummaged through his drawer for trunks, he told me that he only had one rule in his bedroom: If he was naked, everybody had to be. I laughed and pulled off my top and unhooked my bra right then and there. He stepped into these black swim shorts with a red stripe around each leg. They're short—not like board shorts, but nylon and like something you'd see a grown man swim laps in. They weren't a Speedo or anything, but they were trim and tight like him. When he caught sight of me topless, he got this lazy, goofy smile on his face. He said, Damn, these shorts had more room in them before you took off your shirt.

We both collapsed on the bed for a second laughing, and then we kissed and he rolled over on top of me. He kissed my neck and then my breasts and then I pushed him off and said, We have plenty of time to fool around after molly gets here.

And you know what? He said the sweetest thing. He said, You're the only girl I need. I kissed him again on the lips, and then shimmied out of my shorts and into my bikini. As I tucked everything into its proper place up top, Carson just laid on his bed watching me, and when I was all done he said, That's gonna look so good on my floor later. I laughed, arched an eyebrow, and said, If you're lucky.

Then he went over to his nightstand and pulled out a little plastic baggie that had four hits of molly in it. They were the same little capsules that we had taken the other night. He glanced at the clock and did some math. He said it was noon now, so we'd probably just take one and save the other two for another time because his mom would be home by six, and Kyle had said this stuff should give us a good four-hour roll and then we could come down for the last hour from four to five. Then he asked, Swallow or snort?

I tapped my nose, and Carson opened up two capsules and crushed out two beautiful smooth lines on his glass desktop. Then he rolled up a twenty-dollar bill and held it out to me. We both snorted our doses, and then we went into the living room, where he plugged in his iPhone and hit a couple buttons. Music flooded through the house and spilled out into the pool area. Carson handed me a bottle of spray-on waterproof sunscreen, then grabbed a couple of waters from the refrigerator under the bar next to his dad's immense grill.

As soon as we were done with the sunscreen, Carson did a little dive into the deep end of the pool, then swam the length to the shallow end underwater. The sun glinted off his body and he looked like a painting. At the far wall in the shallow end, he did a flip turn like he was an expert swimmer and pushed off the wall, gliding up to the surface in the middle of the pool. He did that thing guys do when they toss their hair as they come up, and the water flinging off his head and sparkling in the sunlight made me feel the first *whoosh* of the molly. It was like he'd tossed diamonds into the air instead of water droplets, and my eyes wiggled with them as they danced across the blue of the sky.

I felt so sexy, standing there in my bikini—like that night at prom. I walked slowly to the edge, and then, without any warning, I did a cannonball off the side with a big yell. When I surfaced, Carson was laughing . . . and holding my bikini top, which had come off as soon as I hit the water. He grinned and said, You're missing something. I kissed him on the lips and took it from him, then tossed it over my shoulder onto the side of the pool and said, How nice for you.

Rolling during the day, outside in the bright sunlight, was different than it usually is. Molly makes me want to dance when there's loud pulsing music and a crowd and a dark dance floor with beautiful lights flashing, but during the day, with Carson, it was a new experience. We floated on the rafts with our bottles of water and smoked a couple cigarettes. We took turns jumping off the side of the pool and feeling the difference on our skin between the hot sun and the cool water. Carson fished a couple of these water cannon tubes out of a bin under the bar. They work like big foam syringes. You suck water into them and then plunge it out. We played with those for at least an hour, lying on rafts watching the trails of light sparkling off the streams of water that he shot into the air. He got really good at doing swirls and curls, and at some point, he kicked off his swim trunks and tossed them onto the side of the pool next to my top. As I write all of this down, I know that it sounds like sort of boring stuff to do, but I can't exactly explain how absolutely exquisite the molly made each of these little things. The visuals created by the sun and water, the light as it played across Carson's body; all of it made me feel completely drenched in pleasure.

I don't remember how long we were out in the water, but I noticed his cheeks—the ones on his face!—were getting a little pink and I said that maybe we should go inside for a while. We toweled off and carried our water bottles and stuff inside. My hair smelled like chlorine so I asked if I could take a shower, and Carson went into his bathroom and started the water. His shower is beautiful. It's not a typical showerhead over a tub; it's a walk-in glass stall with a skylight, and plenty of room for two people. There's a rain-shower showerhead above, and then two additional jets that come out of the wall.

The sex started in the shower, and at some point, we got out and moved onto Carson's bed. When he suggested that we dry off and go someplace more comfortable, I remember feeling relieved because I had the thought that we could get a condom. But when we got onto Carson's bed, the soft sheets against my skin took my breath away, and also the thought of getting a condom. He was kissing me between the legs, and it felt so amazing I couldn't think about anything else. The molly heightened every sensation and seemed to warp time. How it all happened is a little fuzzy in my head now, but at some point, I realized he was inside me. We'd been fooling around for a while, and he is really talented with his tongue down there, so it wasn't this horrible horror story that I'd heard about from other people's first times. Still, it hurt a little and I bled a little even though he went really slowly.

I wonder if I would have said no if I hadn't been rolling. I mean, now, looking back at it, as much as I am into Carson, I'm not sure what's happening with us. It seems silly to pretend that we're going to be together forever in that sort of wide-eyed way that Ashley talks about boys. He's leaving for college in a couple months, and . . . well, I'm not. Also, I didn't want my first time to be on drugs. Something about that felt weird. Plus, I really wish he'd used a condom. Still, he's the sexiest guy I've ever been on a date with—the only handsome one, really—and I would be insane to say no to having a first time with somebody when we have a connection like this, right? It's not that I wish we hadn't had sex. I just wish I hadn't been on molly during it. If I hadn't been, I think I would've at least made sure that he was wearing a condom.

As I was sitting across from Carson at dinner and he was joking around with my dad and making up details about our search for his mom's birthday present, it hit me that Carson didn't even pull out when he finished, and I suddenly got really scared that I might get pregnant. After a minute, I realized that I'd been staring at Ashley. She saw the look on my face, and got this self-satisfied, smug little grin that made me want to reach across the table and smack it off her.

I walked Carson out to his car when he left, and he told me that he had such a good time with me today. Then he said that he loved me. He actually said it. I said that I loved him too, but something really troubles me about the whole experience. I mean, if he really loved me, wouldn't he have worn a condom? Wouldn't he have listened to me when I asked him if he had any instead of just continuing? I don't want to make it seem like he's a bad guy—he's not. I just wish that we hadn't been high.

For the first time, I wish I hadn't done molly.

Wednesday, June 17

I had a really hard time getting to sleep last night. Carson texted me a couple times to say he was thinking about how much fun he had yesterday afternoon, and I guess I finally drifted off sometime this morning around two. When I woke up, I heard Mom walking around the house in her high heels and remembered that she had a meeting with a client early today. She left the house at the same time Dad went to work. As soon as I heard both of their cars pull out of the garage, I went outside and got into mine.

I drove directly to the pharmacy—but not the one we usually go to. I went to one over by the mall, and finally found the Plan B One-Step pills. I had heard about these pills that you could take after you had unprotected sex that would keep any fertilized egg from implanting in your womb, but I couldn't remember what they were called or any of the details about them. I know there was a big fight about it to get them approved because a bunch of people thought they caused abortions. They don't at all. They just keep you from getting pregnant. Anyway, these pills are EXPENSIVE. The ones at the pharmacy by the mall were $49.99 for a single dose. But what choice did I have? I used my debit card to pay for it and was just glad that I was doing this right away. It works best if you take it within seventy-two hours of having unprotected sex, and it hadn't even been twenty-four hours yet.

You'd think that it would be bad enough that I'm having to spend money on this, but as I was walking to the self-checkout register (which I was really glad they had so I didn't have to hand my Plan B pill to a checker and be like, Hi. I'm a huge slut . . .) I came around the corner and ran into Mr. Peterson. Literally. Full-body check. It was possibly the worst experience of my entire life. As I hit him, I of course dropped the Plan B box, and it hit his shoe. He didn't even see who I was before he bent down to pick it up. He was apologizing for running into me, even though I clearly ran into him, and then he froze when he saw what he was picking up.

I probably should have just turned around and run out of the store right then, but it all happened so fast, and before I knew it, I was staring into Mr. Peterson's eyes, or trying not to actually, while he handed me my morning-after birth-control pill. When something this horrifying happens, why can't adults just leave it alone? Why do they have to make it 100,000 times worse? I tried to just head toward the register, but Mr. Peterson reached out and touched my arm and launched into this whole speech about how it was really good to see me and how he has been worried about me, and how sorry he is that the school came down so hard on me. He said that he could probably try to pull a few strings to get me back onto the trip to New York in the fall so I could march in the parade. Finally I just held up my hand and stopped him.

I told Mr. Peterson that I didn't miss band. That I didn't need his help. That I just needed him to stop talking so that I could go home. He blinked at me and nodded, then got all flustered and red-faced and turned around and walked away. I paid at the self-checkout and bought a bottle of water, too. When I got outside, I tore open the box, swallowed the pill, glanced over the instructions, then threw away all the evidence: packaging, receipt, everything.

As I got into my car, Carson texted me. He asked if I wanted to meet him for a coffee and a doughnut. I'm smiling just remembering how sweet he was to me this morning when I got there. I told him what had just happened, and he felt really terrible. I said I'd had my embarrassing trip to the pharmacy and now it was his turn. He blushed, and apologized, and promised to get condoms on the way home.

I can't believe all of this has happened. I mean, if you'd told me two months ago that the band geek with the clarinet would be rolling her ass off and taking Plan B because she had unprotected sex with her hot boyfriend—or whatever he is—I'd have told you that you were nuts. And yet, here I am. The wild child. Mom would be so proud.

Sunday, June 22

It was Derrick's birthday last night and Reid and Carson decided that we should all roll together. Sara was there with Reid, and Kelly joined us even though Jess is boycotting. It was fun to be back at Derrick's house with the whole gang, but I really missed Jess. Kelly and I talked about it a little bit, and she seemed to think that it would all work out eventually. They haven't really been hanging out so I asked if they were officially broken up, and Kelly told me that they'd never officially said that they were girlfriends.

I know what that feels like for sure.

Carson and I have had sex a couple more times since that day we rolled—both times not on drugs, and using condoms. Having sex is fun, and I think I am pretty good at it—or at least getting good at it. Carson says it's the best sex of his life. Of course, he's only had sex with three other girls—or at least that's what he says. He says he loves me, but I'm not sure what our relationship is really about. Part of me is fine with that—realistic about it. The other part feels myself growing more attached and sort of depressed about it. I guess that's why it feels so nice to be on molly with Carson. When we're rolling together, nothing else matters. It's just him and me and there's no problem. I get the overwhelming sensation that everything will be just fine between us—no matter what. That even if he goes off to college, and we both fall in love with other people, things will work out just fine.

It's only the next morning, when I'm sitting here writing in this damn diary, that I wonder if I'm completely full of shit. Will I just fall apart when he leaves?

Friday, June 26

Carson and I went to see a movie yesterday afternoon, and afterward he wanted to go by Reid's place. I'd never been to Reid's house before, and when we got there, Sara was on her way over. She has an internship at a law office downtown this summer. She showed up wearing this black suit with a short skirt and a slim black blazer. Her high heels made her legs look about three hundred feet long. She looked like a lawyer on a TV show—very sophisticated, Reid said. He decided that we should all have sophisticated drinks to match her outfit and started making martinis.

I'd never had a martini and I thought it was kind of gross, so Carson made me a cosmo, which tasted a lot better but got me totally buzzed because it was mainly vodka. We were all hanging out when Reid's dad came home. He actually joined us for a drink. What is it like to have parents like this? My dad would freak out if he came home and found me and Ashley making drinks with a bunch of friends.

After a little while, Kelly showed up in Kyle's big SUV and drove us to this club called The Edge. The music was awesome, and she had molly on her. We all dosed in the car and then went in to the most awesome music I'd heard since the Whip5mart concert. Kyle can DJ like nobody's business. Kelly said that some major labels were talking to him about sending in his EPs and stuff, but Kyle says he can make more money getting on the DJ circuit and selling his mixes on iTunes while he's in college.

Before I left the car, I texted Mom to tell her that I was staying over at Kelly's last night, but I actually ended up at Carson's place. His dad is gone for a week on a business trip to New York, and his mom has gone to Florida to visit her mother for the week, so we had the place to ourselves. We all ended up coming down in Carson's hot tub. After his set at The Edge, Kyle was on his way over to Carson's place, and stopped at home to drop off his gear. While he was there, he nabbed a couple of really good bottles of champagne from his parents' wine fridge.

Reid passed around a bowl in the hot tub and it really helped me get sleepy as I was coming off the molly. Kelly announced that she was going out with Jess tomorrow night, and it made me excited to think that maybe Jess would hang out with us again soon. I really miss her.

This morning when Carson dropped me off, he kissed me and I wondered out loud if we were rolling too much. He smiled and said, I've told you before: You're my girl. I don't need molly around to have fun.

We decided to just go out to dinner this weekend—only the two of us.

Sunday, June 29

I'm so pissed off right now. I don't know whether to be more annoyed with myself or Carson. It's not really his fault, I guess, but it makes me sick to my stomach to think about what happened last night.

Carson came and picked me up at seven just like he promised. He came in and saw my parents and I reminded them that I was going over to Kelly's tonight to spend the night after Carson and I went out. I had zero intention of doing that, but Kelly said it was okay if I told them that.

So, we went to dinner. We had a great time. Just the two of us. We didn't even drink or smoke a bowl beforehand. Carson surprised me and took me to this cool Korean barbecue place where there was a grill in the middle of the table and they bring you raw meat and all the fixings, and you cook it yourself. I had never done anything like that before, and it was really delicious. What was even better than the food was the way that Carson and I got along. I mean, we usually get along and everything, but this was something more. I felt like he was actually my boyfriend last night. He talked about heading to college near San Francisco, and actually talked about me coming up to visit.

Part of me knows that the minute he sets foot on that campus, he's going to be accosted by at least 100,000 college girls, and I have a feeling he won't even look back. But there's this part of Carson that is so painfully sincere, and that was the part that was talking over dinner. I didn't suddenly, unrealistically, hope that we'd be together forever, but Carson was so honest about his feelings that it made me feel special.

Is that lame? I don't care. Carson talked to me about how special I am to him and had all these specific things about me that he loved and appreciated, and no, they weren't all body parts.

This part of last night was so great that it makes me so upset and shaken up about what happened afterward. I guess it's not unusual that Kelly left me a message and said we should come over to her house. Kyle was having a few friends over for drinks and spinning some tunes before they went to this big club downtown. It was a twenty-one-and-over club so the rest of us couldn't get in, but we decided to go hang out with Kelly for a little bit before we went back to Carson's place.

When we got there, Reid and Sara showed up too. We all had some drinks. Carson made me cosmos again and was hanging all over me. He had his arm draped around me the whole night. I had two cosmos and was feeling pretty blitzed when Kyle and all of his friends headed to the club. I was feeling great, so when Kelly brought out the molly, I was all about it.

Carson actually looked at me and asked, Are you sure?

I yelled, HELL YES, and he laughed. But looking back, I was a complete fool. I think Carson would've rather gone back to his house and spent the night just the two of us. Instead, we dropped molly.

Kelly had a shit ton of it because Kyle had just gotten a bunch, and we all snorted two points right away. This was about ten thirty p.m., and around two thirty a.m., Kelly decided that we should all do a third. This amped us back up into the stratosphere until about five a.m. We had plenty of water going, and a ton of great music. Kelly put on a whole show for us with glow sticks and some new black lights that Kyle had.

The thing I'm pissed off about is hard for me to even write down. Carson and I were making out in the hot tub as we were coming down. We'd been smoking some cigarettes out by the pool, and then got back in the hot tub, and he slid an arm around me. When I felt his biceps behind my head, I turned into him and cuddled my chin into that little space between his massive shoulder muscle and his neck. My head fit perfectly, and I wrapped a leg around him under the jets. When I did, I felt that he was hard as a rock, and reached down and gently squeezed. He laughed into our kiss and we decided to move inside.

Sara and Reid were lying on the big shag rug in the den. The TV was on and they had it hooked up to some graphics that were streaming from Kyle's laptop. Some kind of screen saver where the graphics danced along to the beat of the music. Carson and I lay down on the big sectional and started making out again. We were really getting into it, when I felt hands and arms and legs everywhere. It took me a minute to realize that Sara had gotten on the couch behind me and was kissing my neck and back. We were all in various stages of undress, but Carson and I had just been naked in the hot tub and had wrapped up in towels when we came inside, so we were naked in pretty short order.

Here's the thing: Sara is a really pretty girl, but if you'd asked me when I was sober if I wanted to make out with her, I'd have been like, Uh, no. It's not that there's anything wrong with that, it's just I'm not into girls. But all of a sudden, there's Sara kissing my neck from behind. Her bra is off and her breasts are pressed up against my back, and as I open my eyes, I see Carson catch a glimpse of the two of us, and the look in his eyes totally turned me on. I wanted to climb onto him right then and there, but I decided I'd give him a little show. Plus, it was sort of pleasant kissing Sara, so I just decided to go with it.

So I turned to Sara and really started making out with her. Our breasts were rubbing up against each other and stuff, and it was getting me really turned on feeling how hard Carson was. He'd scooted up behind me on the couch when I turned around to make out with Sara, and I could feel he was so hard and had pulled down the towel and was rubbing against me, teasing me from behind. It all felt perfect, so I just backed up against him, and I heard him let out a big breath as he pushed into me.

I just sort of lost myself in it. Having Carson inside of me and feeling his hands running up and down my chest as Sara kissed my mouth and neck . . . the pleasure just coursed through me, wave after wave. I don't even know how long we'd been having sex, but at some point I opened my eyes and saw Carson smiling at me, staring into my eyes with so much love, and as I pressed back again for the next thrust, I realized that it wasn't Carson behind me anymore. I was staring at Carson, and Reid was inside me. Sara's head was buried between Carson's legs, and he was pulling me close again, kissing me. At first I was alarmed, but that's the thing about molly—you can't really hang on to the negative stuff, especially if anything physical is happening to your body. Every sensation is amped up to one hundred times one hundred, and even as I tried to wiggle away from Reid, I could feel him being turned on by it, and I was turned on by the fact that he was turned on. I mean, my body was turned on, but my brain was trying to put the pieces together. Something was wrong. I tried to say "wait" and "no" and "stop," but did I actually say any of those things? I can't remember. All I remember is Carson pulling me toward him, feeling his breath on my ear as he told me how beautiful I was and how amazing this felt.

Then we were all crying out with pleasure—first Carson, his whole body shuddering again and again as Sara finished him off. The sound of his voice and the feel of his arms quaking around me sent me into another spasm of moans, and as

I bucked against Reid, I felt him finish in a fit of jerks and groans.

Afterward, we all collapsed in a pile. We wound up back in the hot tub watching the sun come up, laughing and blissed out and smoking pot and cigarettes. Luckily Kelly was already in her bedroom. A few hours ago, I woke up around noon in Carson's bed, and all I could think about was Reid behind me, moaning as he finished, and I felt like I was going to throw up. Carson dropped me off back at home, and I didn't even go inside. I just got in my car and drove back to the drugstore for more Plan B. This is NOT the way this stuff is suppose to be used. I know it. I'm supposed to be responsible enough to actually use condoms. I mean, if I'm adult enough to have sex, I should be adult enough to do it safely, right?

The worst part of all this is that Carson was so silent when he dropped me off. He gave me a kiss good-bye, but things were so great between us when we left the restaurant last night, and now this . . . I just think this has fucked everything up. Everything I felt from him, the respect, and his sweetness, and all of that— did I just kill that by having group sex with him? How can he respect that?

How can *I* respect that?

ARGH. I am so ANGRY at myself for not saying something. Fucking Reid. And what about Carson? It can't be all my fault, right? He was there too. When did he decide to switch with Reid? Whose idea was that? And why am I the one who feels guilty about it? I didn't ever say "YES" to having sex with Reid. Did I even have the opportunity to say no?

Later...

Mom and Ashley were out shopping or something this afternoon and I wandered into the kitchen to get something to eat. Dad was standing at the sink staring out the window into the backyard. He turned and looked at me and gave me the sweetest smile. There was something so loving and so sad in his eyes that I just started crying.

He walked over to me and put both arms around me and just held me there in the kitchen for what seemed like the longest time. He didn't say a word, he just held me. I felt the warmth of his face against my hair as he pressed his lips to the top of my head. I cried until I couldn't anymore, and as my sobs subsided, Dad handed me a glass of water and asked me if there was something I'd like to talk about.

I wanted to tell him everything. I wanted to tell him so badly. I wanted to tell him all about Carson and Reid and what had happened last night at Kelly's. I wanted to tell him how good it felt to do molly, and how bad it felt to not be sure about what happened last night.

Dad stood there and waited for a long time. I drank my water and handed the glass back to him. As he took it he smiled that sad smile again and said that he remembered a time when I told him all of my secrets.

I guess that time is long gone now. I could never tell my dad any of this. I could never tell anyone any of this.

As good as it feels to roll, as much fun as I have doing molly, I'm beginning to wonder if it's worth it. I mean, I just had unsafe sex again—with a whole group of people. I don't know where Reid has been or what Sara has been up to at college. And regardless of whether my body felt good during the whole experience, my brain was in a different place. Molly can make my body feel good at times when I feel like I should be questioning what's really going on.

I've sent Carson a few texts, but I haven't heard back, which is unlike him and makes me really upset. I wonder if he hates me or thinks I'm a scum ball now. I wonder if he thinks I'm a dirty slut. Screw him if he does. He's the one who kept telling me how good it felt. Why is it that I would call myself a slut and not him?

Monday, June 30

I just got back from seeing Jess for the first time in what seems like forever. She was sort of wary of me at first, but she warmed up as we talked. I still haven't heard back from Carson. This is the first time we've gone without at least texting each other for a full twenty-four hours since prom. It feels so weird.

I told Jess that Carson has become more than a boyfriend— he's actually a really good friend to me now. I didn't tell her about the group sex right then, but I told her about the rest of the sex—even the unsafe first time and the Plan B and running into Mr. Peterson in the pharmacy. She thought that whole story was absolutely brilliant. She laughed so hard, and I started laughing because her laugh is contagious, and we couldn't stop for a long time.

Just like that we were right back to normal. She made us cosmos and we sat out on her patio by the hot tub and drank and talked. She said she's really been missing Kelly, but it was hard for her to see her part in the whole dehydration-at-the-pool dance incident. She said she wanted to blame Kelly, and me, and Carson, but at the end of the day, she was the one who wasn't drinking enough water. I hugged her and got all choked up and told her how sorry I was that I hadn't insisted on going to the hospital with her that night.

I asked her what she was going to do about Kelly, and she shrugged and told me she was going to just take it slow. They have dinner plans tomorrow night, and Jess said she's excited to see her again.

Then Jess turned to me and said, Okay: Spill it. What's eating at you?

I love that it doesn't matter how long we spend apart, Jess knows when I'm not telling her everything. I told her that Carson hadn't been texting me back. I didn't want to tell her that I was afraid it was because we'd had group sex with Reid, but somehow Jess pried it out of me. I swore her to secrecy, and she rolled her eyes at me and said, Really? This is me you're talking to.

I spilled the whole sordid story, and you know what her response was? She looked me straight in the eyes as I cried tiny tears and she said: You skinny bitches have ALL THE FUN.

We cracked up so hard, and as we were gasping for breath, she told me that the reason Carson wasn't texting me back is because he was worried about the fact that his penis and Reid's penis had been naked and hard and so close to each other. I giggled so hard at this and told her that was ridiculous—that Sara and I were full-on making out. Why would the guys be weird about being naked together on opposite sides of me? Jess told me that girl sexuality is way more fluid in our culture than boy sexuality, and she guaranteed me that Carson and Reid were both coming to terms with the fact that they'd been naked together and what that meant.

Jess said that Dr. Kinsey had proven years ago that human sexuality was a continuum. She said, Let's just put it this way: After Saturday night, Reid and Carson are both coming to grips with the fact that they both fall closer to the middle of the curve than they do to the "straight" end of that curve.

And just like that, I had my best friend back.

Tuesday, July 1

Carson FINALLY called me back today.

He apologized for not texting me. Then he came over and we went on a walk around the neighborhood. He said that he wasn't freaked out about the whole group-sex thing. I brought it up right away, and he just held my hand and we talked through it. He said that Reid had initiated the big switch off, and he was still so high on the third hit of molly that he didn't stop Reid. Then he started crying. His eyes filled up with tears at least. He didn't sob like a baby or anything, but he stopped and pulled me close and said that he was so sorry.

That he never meant to hurt me, and it made him so upset that I thought he'd ever want to share me with anybody else—especially Reid.

I took his face in my hands and kissed him right there on the street. I said that this was exactly what I wanted to hear, and all the fear and nervousness of the past couple days slipped away. I said that I was a big girl and I had a responsibility to stick up for myself and say NO when I didn't want something. Molly had made all that fuzzy the other night. We agreed on safe sex from now on. And only sex with the two of us.

When we got back to my house, my mom had made fresh-squeezed lemonade, like someone in a picture book or a movie on Lifetime. Carson blinked at my mother, and said, Your mom is magic. Of course, Mom insisted that he stay for dinner after that.

As we were finishing up dessert, the doorbell rang and I got up to open it. Before I could even say hello, Jess and Kelly burst into the entryway, and Jess practically yelled: Why haven't you answered ANY of my texts? I've been calling and texting for HOURS. Then she saw everyone sitting at the dinner table, and sheepishly waved.

Jess and Kelly had some dessert, and then I went up to my room with them and Carson. Kelly asked Ashley if she was coming, but she settled onto the couch and said that she was going to watch a movie, basically giving Kelly the cold shoulder. She glared at me as I left the room, and I wondered how I would pay for all this later.

Upstairs, Kelly filled us in on the big news: It was just announced that Whip5mart is playing the Flaming Daisy Carnival over the July 4 weekend. Flaming Daisy is this big rave and electronic musical festival at the polo fields on the edge of town. The Whip5mart appearance is a surprise and the festival was already going to be sold out, but Kelly was able to wrangle tickets from her brother's friend who is a big club promoter. Unfortunately, Kyle was only able to get four tickets, and Reid, Sara, Kelly, and Jess are using them. Kelly has already put in a "big order" for molly with her brother, and he was working on finding another couple of tickets for me and Carson.

Carson said it was okay that there wasn't a ticket for him because he has to go on a family vacation next week. Jess said she was just excited about the music because what she remembers of that night at the pool was that the music was off the chain. She said she won't do molly, but Kelly has convinced her to come along anyway. That it will be fun.

I'm really upset that Carson can't come. Even if I can get a ticket, it won't be half as much fun without him. Of course, I've spent over a hundred dollars on birth control in the last month, so even if they find a ticket for me, I probably can't afford it. I didn't actually say that last little detail, but Jess and Kelly were bummed that Carson couldn't come too. Kelly tried to convince me to come without him, but I told her I didn't think I could afford it, and she understood.

After Jess and Kelly left, Carson told me he was leaving with his parents the day after tomorrow. They're all going to Mexico. His dad has some work thing there, so his mom is insisting that they go along so they can have a "family vacation."

He said he wanted to make sure he had me all to himself for dinner tomorrow night. I assured him that he had me all to himself anytime he wanted.

Wednesday, July 2

OH MY GOD, HE'S INCREDIBLE.

All my fears about Carson not being into me when he wasn't texting me back? Well, he totally made up for all that. We went to dinner tonight at a Mexican restaurant. When the waiter brought our food, he dropped off my enchiladas, and then placed a smaller plate next to it and said, And here's your side of Flaming Daisy. I looked at him, confused, and he just smiled and left, and then I looked at the plate and there were TWO

PASSES TO FLAMING DAISY SITTING ON IT! I couldn't believe it!

Carson had gotten phone numbers from Kyle, and spent all day tracking down passes. I don't even want to know how much he paid for them. I was bouncing around in the booth and sort of tackled him on his side before I stopped and asked him about his family vacation. He explained that his dad had gotten called to some big meeting in Taiwan, so they'd had to postpone the Mexico trip. His mom had already changed her tickets to fly to Portland to see her sister for the weekend. She wanted him to come with her, but he told her that he was staying so he could take me to Flaming Daisy instead.

I can't wait for this weekend! Everything kicks off on Friday night. We'll drive down Friday afternoon. There's a big campground on one of the polo fields, and all the music stages and tents are set up on the other polo field. They have trailers with bathrooms and showers at one end of the campground, so you just pitch a tent in the middle of the field, and you're all set for the weekend. Carson has already reserved camping passes for us. We're going to get settled on Friday night, then spend all day Saturday and Sunday seeing bands and DJs play.

Of course, Kelly has a massive order of molly, too, so this is going to be a weekend to remember.

Thursday, July 3

If my sister thinks she can ruin this weekend and make me as miserable as she is, she's wrong. I am so angry I can barely hold my pen. My whole body is shaking. I just yelled at my parents and Ashley and came up to my room and locked the door. My mom was so pissed off at me that she chased me up here and banged on the door and yelled for at least fifteen minutes. If she thinks I'm going to open that door and let her in, she has another thought coming. I am going to the Flaming Daisy Carnival with Carson. And I am going to do molly. And I won't let anything get in my way. Not Ashley and her pathetic whining. Not my parents and their "concern." I am going to feel good and there is nothing they can do to stop me.

This all started because Ashley is jealous of me. She's spent the past month moping around the house feeling sorry for herself and whining about how Reid was a jerk. It wasn't enough for her to feel badly. She has to make EVERYONE feel as badly as she does, so she TOLD MOM AND DAD about how I was still doing molly.

Dad sat down at dinner, and Mom was shockingly quiet and Ashley had this look on her face—I can't explain it, but I just felt this punch right in my gut, and I had this moment where I realized I was about to be ambushed. And then Dad looked at me and said, We need to have a talk about your drug use.

I swear to god that Ashley actually smiled at me across the table when he said it, and I just looked at her and said, You bitch.

Mom gasped like she'd been shot, and then Dad started telling me that my language was unacceptable and that I was not to speak like that to my sister. I told him that I was done trying to pretend that we were some wonderful happy family when it was clear that Ashley and Mom were a team, and Ashley was just jealous of me because Reid had dumped her.

Ashley stood up and pushed her chair back and leaned across the table to yell at me. She told me that Reid had come crawling back to her yesterday because Sara was so pissed off at him about what happened at Kelly's the other night. I just blinked at her and felt like I was going to throw up. I yelled that she needed to shut up, and she just threw her head back and laughed at me. She pointed at Mom and Dad and said, Why? So they don't find out about your little four-gy? Oh, don't worry, they already know.

I looked at Mom and then at Dad, and they were both stone-faced. Mom looked sort of green and Dad had tears running down his face. God! I am so tired of him crying at the drop of a hat. I was so pissed off at Ashley that I just yelled at her again to shut up, and then she folded her arms across her chest and looked supremely satisfied with herself. She told me that it was too late. That I couldn't shut her up. She said that Sara had gotten wind that Reid was trying to get Ashley back. Sara was so pissed at him that she called Ashley and told her that Reid had screwed me that night at Kelly's house while we were all high on molly—while Carson was watching. Then, to top off this little recap, she shouted at me that Sara had told everyone. Her eyes flashed a strange triumph over me at the dinner table as she shouted, Now everyone knows you're a TOTAL SLUT.

When she said that, I picked up my water glass and threw the entire thing at her head. She got drenched with water, but dodged the glass. It hit the edge of the stool at the kitchen counter behind her and shattered into a million pieces. Dad stood up and roared at the two of us to BE QUIET THIS INSTANT.

Dad looked at me with so much anger and hurt in his eyes. He told me that he wanted me to go to my room and that I would not be doing anything with Carson ever again, or even leaving the house without him or my mom for the rest of the summer. He said that they'd called several recovery centers and that tomorrow afternoon we had an appointment at one of them so that we could talk to a counselor about my "addiction."

I just laughed at him, and my mom said that this was NO LAUGHING MATTER, which just made me think the entire thing was even funnier. Please. Like I'm the one who has a problem. I said this and then told them that Ashley was the one with all the problems and she just couldn't stand the idea that I actually had a hot boyfriend who loved me, and a great group of friends, and that I could handle partying a little without losing my freaking mind and gushing all over a teacher—which is how we got into this freaking mess in the first place.

Dad tried to shout me down and tell me that I was wrong about all of this—that I had some sort of drug problem. I told him he didn't know what the hell he was talking about. Molly isn't physically addictive. I told him to go online and at least do a little research before he started throwing around terminology he didn't understand. I've done plenty of research online. The people on that forum talk about this all the time—how they can quit anytime they want to with no physical withdrawal symptoms.

Dad didn't want to hear any of this. I told him that I wasn't addicted at all. He said that he was glad to hear it because that meant I could quit and I'd be just fine. I laughed and said, Oh, I COULD quit, but I don't WANT to.

He shook his head and said, You are not going to the Flaming Daisy Carnival this weekend.

I just smiled at him and said, TRY TO STOP ME.

Then I marched up here to my room and locked the door.

If these crazy fuckers think they can stop me from going to that festival, they don't know me very well.

Friday, July 4
Happy INDEPENDENCE DAY, BITCHES!

I bet there will be some fireworks when Mom figures out I gave her the slip. She got into the shower this morning after Ashley went for a run, and Dad had gone to his office to pick up some health insurance information so he could give it to whatever drug rehab counseling place they were going to take me to. Fuck that. I texted Carson and told him that I needed to get out of here. I told him a little about Ashley and Reid and Sara and that my parents had found out. He parked down the block, and while Mom was in the shower, I left. I locked my bedroom door and pulled it closed behind me, so that'll buy me a little time.

Carson is in the shower right now and then we're going to pack up his truck with the tent and sleeping bags and stuff. We're going to drive down to the polo fields early and stake out a good camping spot, then Kelly and Jess are coming down with Kyle and a group of his friends later this afternoon.

My parents will be pissed, but what can they really do to me? I'm not some child anymore. I'm turning eighteen in a few months. I can make my own decisions. I can certainly go to hear some bands and DJs play. I can't wait do some molly and dance to Whip5mart with Carson again. There's nothing else like that in the world.

Saturday, July 5

This place is OFF THE HOOK. There must be over 100,000 people here. I seriously have NEVER seen so many people in one place in my entire life. The crowds have spilled out of the camping area and people are just setting up tents in the empty fields for what looks like miles around. When Carson and I got here to set up the tents, it was already packed. There are some FREAKS here, and I mean that in the BEST POSSIBLE WAY!

We are all getting ready to go into the music festival. Last night there was this big bonfire, and people were in all of these crazy costumes running around on stilts and swinging fire on chains. There's this wild contingent of people who are all in costumes all the time. Kyle and his friends nabbed the area next to us. When Reid and Sara showed up I was prepared. I walked right up to them and said, I don't want there to be a big dramatic scene. Sara smiled and gave me a hug. She said she was sorry about calling Ashley. I told her that it wasn't our family's finest moment, but that we'd all survive.

Then Kelly said, Yeah, but only if your dad doesn't find you now.

I was like, WHAT THE HELL ARE YOU TALKING ABOUT? Jess said that he was standing out at the gates to the camping area when they arrived. He didn't see them because there are so many people. You have to have a special pass to get into the camping area, and you have to have a pass to get into the event space where the music is. I'm sure Dad didn't spend the night here last night, and there's no way he could actually find me in all these people. Still, it makes my stomach feel jumpy. I actually feel sort of bad for him. I know he must be really upset, but I'm not going to let him ruin this weekend for me.

Carson is sitting crossed-legged on his sleeping bag next to me while I write. He's splitting up our doses from the baggie that Kyle gave him this morning. We decided to wait to roll until the sun goes down, so we're just smoking some pot this morning, and Kyle got us all special purple wristbands so we can get beer even though we're not twenty-one yet. We want to save rolling for when it cools down a little, and Whip5mart doesn't start spinning until ten tonight. But there is PLENTY of fun to be had before then. Jesus. Just staring at Carson walking around in his tennis shoes and cutoffs is enough to keep me occupied. He's got a baseball cap on and his tank top is already hanging from his belt loops.

This is gonna be a scorcher—mainly because he's so HOT!

Sunday, July 6

It's so weird to sit in a tent in the middle of thousands of people and have it be so quiet. It's about nine a.m. and I just woke up. We didn't come down until around six a.m., so I should be more tired than I am, but I feel energized and . . . alive. Something about this experience has been magic. I finally feel like I'm free—like I'm an adult for the first time. I'm not afraid to just be who I am. Yesterday, we saw so many great bands and I was with the hottest guy at this festival. Carson held my hand and walked around with me the whole day and we had the BEST TIME. We met these gay guys, Trent and Matty, dancing in the tent where Krystal Whip was spinning a set, and they were awesome. They were saving their molly, too, but they gave us each a bump of coke and it got us grooving and moving. Their bodies were hot like Carson's, and they thought I was awesome, and they LOVED Jess. Reid was a little weirded out by them at first and didn't want to dance near them, but Carson told him to chill, and he snapped out of it. Carson is so funny—he totally got between Trent and Matty and dirty danced with them. They loved it, and who wouldn't? Carson is smoking hot and completely comfortable with who he is—which is one of the reasons that I think he's just freaking attractive to EVERYBODY.

We all ended up dancing together for a long time, and once

the sun went down, Matty and Trent came back to our tent, and we did a couple points of molly each, then headed back to the festival and got in position for the Whip5mart set. There were a couple bands before he went on, and they were great, but when Whip5mart took the stage, the place went OFF THE HOOK. There was a laser light show that was amazing. It was like being on a different planet—or in the middle of a sci-fi movie. Carson and I danced like we'd never danced before. We'd all brought a bunch of water jugs, the big gallon ones, so we wouldn't have to leave our spots up by the stage, and it was a good thing we did, because nobody felt like leaving to go stand in line for more water.

We were having so much fun that Carson wanted to do a little more molly to keep the high going while we danced. Matty and Trent were out, so we decided to share the two hits that we had left with them. Carson was able to dump the capsules out on his phone screen and then we carefully snorted half a line each. It gave us the perfect little pick-me-up around two a.m.

It turns out that Whip5mart is going to play again tonight. It was a surprise that they announced last night. While we were coming down a few hours ago, Matty told us that he had more molly to share as a thank-you for splitting our points with him and Trent. Kelly said she was worried about taking their molly because it wasn't tested and we weren't sure exactly what we'd be getting, but Kyle's running low—mainly because he's sold so much over the past couple nights. I'm sure it'll be fine.

I'm getting a little tired again right now, and I'm sure everybody will start waking up around the camp within the next hour. Carson is snoring lightly and he's so CUTE the way he sleeps with his arms thrown up over his head. I'm going to snuggle in next to him and see if I can get another twenty minutes or so before this whole place wakes up and becomes another all-day crazy party.

I could get used to living like this. Just me and Carson and some good friends, some great music, and some awesome molly.

Later...

I HATE MY PARENTS! I hate them! They suck! They suuuuuuuck!!!! Oh my god, oh my god, I've never been so humiliated in my entire life. I can't I can't I can't.

Okay, I had to step away for a few minutes and catch my breath. My hands were shaking so hard. But I still can't believe what happened today. I can't. How could my dad do that to me? The cops?!?! I mean, what am I, a mass murderer or something? The cops?!

Let me start at the beginning. It was around two o'clock

or so. I'm not totally sure because we'd been rolling most of the day, but I know the sun was frickin' hot so it was probably midafternoon. Me and all my friends were lying in the grass, looking up at the clouds. My head was on Carson's chest and he was playing with my hair. Jess's head was in my lap and Kelly's legs were hooked over hers and there were a few other people there too, but I can't really remember who. All I know is, we were all woven together on the ground like some perfect tapestry, and I remember thinking how amazing it would be if someone could actually make a fabric out of all of us. How beautiful that would be. Because my friend's hearts are so beautiful.

I know. It sounds dorky now, but then it just felt so profound. So, there we were, pointing out shapes in the clouds—I mean, how much more innocent can you get than that?—when suddenly there was my dad's shadowy face looking down at me. And behind him were two cops in full uniform.

I was so high that I threw my arms up and smiled and *might* have yelled, Daddy! Carson sat up so fast he gave me whiplash.

Is this the man who kidnapped your daughter, sir? the fat cop asked.

WHAT?!?!

Kidnapped? Carson said, pulling a T-shirt on over his perfect abs. Nobody kidnapped anyone.

I struggled to my feet, still trying to understand what was going on. I noticed that all around me people were shoving stuff in bags and some of them were running for the gates. One second, everything was peaceful and beautiful. Then my dad walks in and BAM! Festival over.

The cop had Carson's bicep in one hand. He asked my dad if he wanted to press charges. My father said no. He just wanted to take his daughter out of here.

Then the cop stepped up to me and was all like, Miss? Have you ingested any illegal substances today? And I just started laughing. I couldn't help it. He was so, so, so serious and his face was all puffy and red.

My dad pulled the cop aside. A couple seconds later, someone announced that we weren't pressing charges, and then my dad dragged me out of there. Dragged me out by my arm, like some kind of criminal. I shot Carson a look over my shoulder, but he just stared back at me, stunned. He was so high I'm not even totally sure he could see me. But I needed to say good-bye to him at least. I needed to kiss him. I yanked my arm away from my dad and tried to run back, but he just grabbed me by both arms this time, pinning them to my sides, and half carried, half dragged me the rest of the way. I never knew my dad was that strong.

I kept yelling at him that I didn't want to go and that this was where I belonged, and the more I yelled, the more purple his face got. At the gates, people were streaming out, terrified of the cops, I guess. The cops my father had brought to the festival. He practically threw me in the car and slammed the door.

He didn't talk to me all the way home, but I sure talked to him. I told him this was my life and those people really cared about me, and I wanted to be with them and not him or my mom or Ashley. I don't think he heard one word of it, though. By the time we got back I had definitely come down from my last dose of molly. The adrenaline must have washed it out of my system. My dad opened my door, and I got out before he could manhandle me some more. I stormed into the house and my mom was in the foyer. She took one look at me, and started crying. I rolled my eyes and stomped upstairs. My dad followed me into my room and told me to shower.

What are you, my warden? I demanded.

He said yes, basically, he was.

That was when I screamed. I screamed so loud I swear the house shook. He flinched, but he didn't move. I went into the bathroom and took off my clothes and a hit of molly fell out of my bra. It was sweaty, but the tissue baggy was in tact. I couldn't even remember who I'd gotten it from. Trent and Matty? Kyle? I wasn't sure. But I quickly hid it inside a bottle of Midol in my medicine cabinet, then got in the shower. When I came out in my robe, my dad was waiting for me. I couldn't believe it. He'd just stood there the whole time. Like, what? I was gonna Hulk out and punch a hole through the bathroom wall to escape?

He told me that I wasn't leaving my room without one of my parents for the next two weeks. Not the house. My *room*. When I tried to protest, he said I'd brought this upon myself. He said something about bringing my dinner up later, then walked out, and closed the door. And here's the best part—I heard a *click*.

I glanced at the door and saw that there was a new doorknob on it. All fake-gold and shiny. I grabbed it and turned, and nothing happened. MY PARENTS LOCKED ME IN MY ROOM! Yes, while I was gone for two days having a perfectly fun and safe time with my friends, my parents were out shopping for a new doorknob so they could lock me up like some kind of wild animal. I've spent the last hour on the internet trying to find out if this is even legal, but apparently it's a gray area.

But I don't care. I am never speaking to them again. NEVER! And if Carson breaks up with me for this, I'm leaving. They want to track my every move? Well, let's see how they like it if they never see me again.

Monday, July 7

Just when you think things can't get any worse, they do. I'm writing this right now in my room where there is nothing but my bed, my dresser, my computer, my clarinet, my phone, and this journal. My parents took every other thing out of my room this afternoon and put it god knows where. I'm living in a cell.

Also I've texted Carson ten times and he hasn't texted me back. If he's in jail right now because of my dad, I'm seriously going to kill someone. I'm so angry. I honestly think I could punch my father in the face. I really do. I never thought I could be this angry at him. This is my dad. He's always on my side. But whatever. That's over now, I guess.

At least Jess is okay. We've texted some, and she's grounded, too. Parents are so predictable. But anyway, back to the insanity.

Here's how it all went down. This morning both my parents walked into my room fully showered and dressed at nine a.m. and told me to get up and get dressed. We were meeting with the substance-abuse therapist.

I told them, Great. Have fun. And pulled my blankets over my head.

My dad ripped them off of me. He said, very sternly, that he and my mother loved me and they weren't going to watch me destroy my life. Apparently they *were* going to watch me get dressed, though, because my mom stood there while I got completely naked and put on a new underwear and bra. Then I yanked a T-shirt and sweatpants on, and shoved my feet into flip-flops. The whole time, I kept waiting for her to tell me this was a joke. Tell me not to worry about it. That they still trusted me. But it never happened. They were really going through with this. They were really going to drag me to some stranger to talk about how I, what? Liked to have fun? I'm seventeen. I'm supposed to be having fun, right?

My heart was pounding as I looked at my mom. Do we really have to do this? I asked. Please? I won't sneak out again, I swear.

Her mouth was so thin it was practically not even there. She told me not to try begging my way out of this, which just pissed me off. She always caved when Ashley got all cute and weepy and pleading. I went into the bathroom and slammed the door.

What're you doing? my mother demanded.

God! Can't I even pee?

I heard her huff, and then she said I had two minutes. I peed and then realized my mouth tasted like ass, probably from all the pot and molly and junk food I'd ingested the past couple of days. I opened the medicine cabinet to get my toothpaste, and the Midol bottle stared at me. I took it out, and opened it up. The hit of molly was nestled in there all safe and sound. I closed the cabinet again, and stared at myself in the mirror. I'd never done molly outside of a party situation. I'd never done it without my friends. And if my parents figured it out, they'd kill me. But honestly, they'd already locked me in my room. How much worse could it get? (If only I knew.)

Screw them, I thought. There was only one way to survive this torture, and that was to be high.

I ran the water, tossed the packet into the back of my mouth, and drank it down.

Just brushing my teeth, Warden! I shouted for my mom's benefit.

She was waiting for me, of course.

Before we left the house, I grabbed a bottle of water from the fridge. Gotta stay hydrated. And they think I'm not responsible. My parents were silent in the front seat of the car. I sat in the back by myself and waited for the molly to kick in. Which it did pretty much the second we walked into this totally posh office building downtown. I mean, honestly? These substance-abuse people must make a crap load of money. Everything was plush and gold and marble, and the lobby was superhushed and supremely air-conditioned. Right in the middle of the lobby was this wall of cascading water burbling over cut glass, and I was totally distracted by the sunlight beaming off of it in all directions. It was like being inside a rainbow, and I remember thinking, I wish Carson and Jess were here to see this.

Actually, I might have said it out loud, because my mom looked at me kind of funny. Then my dad announced that we were going to the fifth floor, and we got on the elevator. That was a totally mind-boggling experience, by the way. As soon as we went up, I felt like I was standing on my head, and by the time we got off, I was dizzy. Elevators and molly do not mix.

I blearily followed my dad into this mostly white office, and the receptionist buzzed the doctor or whatever you call him. While we waited, I rubbed the hem of my T-shirt between my thumb and forefinger. It was so soft. I had no idea clothes could be that soft. Then, suddenly, we were up and walking into the counselor's office.

His name was Tim Burbridge, and he had a soul patch. A soul patch! It looked like a little caterpillar dancing its way across his face. I laughed and reached out to touch it with my thumb. It felt surprisingly silky against my skin.

Of course, this was a big mistake.

My mom actually gasped. My dad asked what I was doing. Tim looked me dead in the eye and said, Your daughter is rolling right now.

Which made me laugh some more. Then my mother asked what rolling meant, and that made me laugh even harder.

The next thing I knew, Tim was telling my parents he couldn't treat me when I was like this. That there was a detox facility in the hospital, or they could detox me at home. My mother was so white I thought I might be able to see through her.

We'll take her home, she said. We can handle this. Tim gave them some kind of pamphlet with instructions on what to do. Like I'm their new and exotic pet.

And then I was back in the car and I was victorious. I'd gotten out of substance-abuse therapy. Go me!

Of course, what I probably should've done was ask to see the pamphlet, because when we got home, my parents did every single thing it said to do, line by line. They made me sit in the corner while they searched every inch of my room, even though I kept telling them there were no more drugs. I'm not a junkie, I kept saying, but they didn't listen. They emptied my drawers, my closet, my bedside tables, my desk, under my bed. My mom grabbed this journal, and started to flip through it, but I snatched it away from her, and hugged it to me while they finished their gestapo impression. Then they took everything out. My books, my iPod, my sketch pad, my old stuffed animals. Everything. And then they locked the door again.

So here I am. Stuck for three days straight while I "detox." I swear, they're all so clueless. The molly is already out of my system. I know, because I feel like shit. I don't need three more days to flush anything out. If they knew anything about this drug, they'd know that.

And if they knew anything about me, they'd know there's no way I'm staying in this damn room alone for three whole days.

Tuesday, July 8

I am sooooo tired. I swear I slept almost all day. I only woke up to text with Carson, who was not arrested, but lost his phone somehow at the Flaming Daisy Carnival and had to get a new one. He's fine. His mom talked to my dad and found out that my father only told the cops that Carson had kidnapped me so that they'd break him into the festival. So, no one at Carson's house is very happy with my dad either. His parents are so cool. They just trust him. Whatever. At least he's not mad at me. He just feels bad for me. He thinks my parents have gone off the deep end, and I so agree with him, because get this:

Every once in a while I get up and check if my door is still locked and it is. It's always locked. And every time I try to turn the knob, either my father or my mother instantly says, Do you need something? Yeah. One of them is always sitting right outside my door. Don't they have anything better to do with their time?

Somewhere around noon my head started pounding, like from the inside out. I went into my bathroom for some Tylenol, but it wasn't there. Nothing's there. They took every last thing out of my medicine cabinet, even my floss. Because, why? I might try to hang myself with it? Honestly I think my skull might break, but I refuse to ask them for anything. I'm just going to go back to sleep. They can't stay out there all night, right? Later I'm going to look up how to pick a lock on the internet. God. I can't believe I even just wrote that. I wonder what my parents would think if they knew that they were forcing me to become a criminal mastermind. But later. Right now, I can barely keep my eyes open.

Wednesday, July 9

I just slept for twenty-one hours straight. When I woke up, there was a sandwich and a bottle of water on my nightstand, and I was so starving I wolfed it down and then threw it right back up. I guess when you don't eat for like a day and a half your stomach can't handle that much food at one time. Anyway, I finally had to cave and ask my mom for my toothbrush and toothpaste. She stood in the doorway of the bathroom and watched me brush my teeth, then made me hand the brush and tube back to her.

I feel like I'm broken. My whole body is tired, and I can't even stand up straight. When I looked at my mom, I felt this pathetic impulse. I wanted her to hug me and kiss my forehead like she always does when I puke. But instead, she just gave me her patented look of disappointment, walked out, and locked the door again.

Later, she brought me toast and chicken soup. I refused to eat it. I swear it's like I'm in Guantánamo or something.

Thursday, July 10

I can't take it anymore. I can't. I'm going to lose my mind. I did find out how to pick a lock, but every time I so much as touch that doorknob, one of my parents barks at me. Is this the last day of my incarceration? I think it is, but I'm not sure. I swear if I have to stare at my walls for five more seconds, I'm going to lose it. I really am. I feel like my blood is made of caffeine. I can't stop shaking. Is it a panic attack? I think it's a panic attack. They can't keep me locked up in here anymore. They just can't. I'm texting Jess and Carson. Maybe they can figure out a way to get me out of here.

Later . . .

Oh my god Oh my god Oh my god.

I'm so screwed. My parents caught me climbing out my

window, and now they've taken my phone away too. And I have to go back to therapy tomorrow. And I'll also probably never see my friends again.

I spent half the day texting with Jess and Carson, trying to come up with a plan. Jess wanted to just come over and beg, but I knew that wouldn't work. Not with the state of crazy my parents are currently living in. They knew they couldn't get me out through my door, so then Carson suggested he bring an escape ladder. I think he was actually kidding, but I jumped on it. I mean, my parents are always inside the house, guarding the door. Would anyone really notice if he came over and put a ladder next to my window? The Jensens next door are away for the summer, so there's no one on that side of the house to see. It was the perfect plan. Or so I thought.

Carson knew that if he stepped foot on my yard, my dad would call the cops and this time he wouldn't get off with a warning, so he sent Reid. I didn't exactly love the idea of getting rescued by him, but I was so desperate at that point, I didn't care. Plus, Reid is turning out to be the guy who's up for anything, which I guess makes him a good person to have around. Sometimes, anyway.

We decided to wait until ten o'clock, because I'd figured out that that was when my mom took over so my dad could go watch the news, probably. If Reid could get there right when my parents were having their nightly update about how my life is going down the toilet and what they can do to control me, then they might be too distracted to hear anything. I swear, time passed more and more slowly as we headed toward ten p.m., but then, finally, it was here, and Reid was right on time. I saw his truck turn onto our street, and he even turned off his headlights like he was in some spy movie.

The sound of the ladder hitting the house seemed deafening to me, but my door didn't open. I slid the window up as quietly as I could and looked down. Reid grinned up at me.

S'up Rapunzel? he whispered.

I rolled my eyes. The drop suddenly seemed so far, but this was the only way. My heart pounded like crazy as I put one foot out, then the other. The ladder was pretty steady, but I was still terrified as I started down it. Every second I expected to hear one of my parents shout at me from above, but they never did, and then, I was on the ground. I grinned at Reid and ran for his truck.

The ladder! he whisper-shouted.

Leave it! I cried back. Just get me out of here!

I was just racing around the front of the house when my sister opened the front door with a book in her hand. Going to read on the porch swing like the picture of perfection she is. She took one look at me and I froze. I pleaded with her with my eyes and for half a second, I was sure she was going to take pity on me and let me go. Then, Reid came around the corner.

Mom! Ashley screeched. Mom! Dad! Get out here!

And the rest is history. I'm locked in my room again, and now I can't even text my friends.

I fucking hate Ashley.

Monday, July 14

I've been out of the house twice since my last entry, both times to counseling with Mr. Soul Patch. He wants me to call him Tim, so I call him Mr. Burbridge. So far, I haven't said anything to him. Not one word aside from "Hello, Mr. Burbridge" and "Bye, Mr. Burbridge." My mom goes in to chat with him after the sessions. When she comes out, she looks more pissed off than I've ever seen her and won't speak to me on the way home. There's a lot of not speaking going on around here in general.

So, get this, I'm allowed out of my room. Know why? Over the weekend, my parents had a new alarm system installed and every time you open a window or a door, it announces which window or door has been opened. Yeah. I'm officially living in a loony bin.

Also I officially have no life. The first thing I did when I got back from counseling was check my e-mail to see if Jess or Carson responded to the rants I sent them this morning. Neither one of them did.

Wednesday, July 16

I'm so bored! Honestly, how much reality TV can one person watch before their brain melts? I keep trying to read, but whenever I start, my mind wanders and I realize I've read the same sentence ten times, or that I've been staring at the wall for ten minutes thinking about nothing. I'm so bored that I actually talked to Mr. Soul Patch this morning. He asked me how I was feeling and I said, Like shit.

So, he asked if I wanted to elaborate on that, and I said, Runny, mushy, smelly shit?

I expected him to get angry, but he laughed.

We talked for like five more minutes after that, mostly about how pissed off I was, because that's all I feel. Angry. All the time. I don't understand what my parents are so fricking tense about. So I went to a few parties. Obviously I'm not addicted to anything or I'd be jonesing for a fix right now, right? That's the thing about molly. It's NOT ADDICTIVE! Why doesn't anybody get that? Why won't they let me make my own decisions?

I've been a good girl my whole entire life, never stepped a foot out of line, and the one time I try to have a little fun everyone goes apeshit crazy. It's so not fair.

So, I said all this to Soul Patch, and he said, You don't understand why your parents are worried about you? Why they're afraid for you?

My jaw clenched, and I said, no. I wish they'd just get the eff off my back.

He wasn't smiling anymore when he said the session was over.

Friday, July 18

I got an e-mail from Jess today. First one in four days. She got a job at the Dairy Queen for the rest of the summer, so I guess she's busy. I guess Carson's busy too, because I barely hear from him and when I do it's like one line about something he did that day or where he's going next. They're all free. They're all out there having lives. No one cares that my life is over. No one cares about me.

I got so bored today that I tried to play my clarinet, but I couldn't get into it. I put it back in the case, and shoved it into the back of my closet. For the last three hours, I've been lying here, staring at the ceiling. It's like I can't get into anything.

Not playing, not reading, not even Candy Crush. Nothing's fun anymore. Even writing this is making me bored. It's five o'clock and sunny as anything outside. I can hear kids playing down the street, shrieking and laughing. I don't think I've ever felt so sad.

Friday, July 25

I miss my friends. I miss school. I can't even believe it's summer. Somewhere out there people are swimming. They're at the beach, they're having barbecues, they're going to concerts. I miss having something to do other than listen to fucking Soul Patch and hear my parents sigh. I don't think I can do this much longer. I really don't.

Saturday, July 26

Okay, this has been the weirdest day. I don't even know where to start. But my parents let me out of the house. Alone. I know. I couldn't even believe it. It was mostly my father, really. He took pity on me. He said he couldn't take my sad face anymore. And I guess he can tell I'm not some crazed addict, since I haven't had a hit of molly in over two weeks and I haven't started seizing or tried to kill anyone for drug money. Anyway, Jess called and asked him if I could come over, and he said yes. Later she told me she actually dropped the phone.

So, okay. Before I left, he told me I was to go straight to Jess's and come straight home and that, of course, I wasn't to touch drugs or alcohol. He said he was trusting me. And then he gave me the car keys.

Woo-hoo! I'd never been so excited in my whole life. I swear, driving over to Jess's, everything looked different. It was all brighter and sharper somehow. I felt like I'd just come out of a coma or something.

Anyway, the first thing Jess did after hugging me for like five minutes was tell me that Kelly's friend Jasmine was having a party. Her parents were out of town and she had a pool with a swirly slide and everything, and I was like, I'm in. She only lives five minutes away and swimming seemed like an awesome idea. I'd worn a bathing suit under my clothes so we could lie out in the backyard, so I was good to go.

When we got there, it was totally clear that half the people at the party were rolling. People were making out in the pool or chasing one another around the yard with these huge bubble wands, popping monster bubbles with their tongues. One guy on a lounge chair was rubbing lotion onto a girl's back and looked like he was in heaven. Everyone was having so much fun, but I felt this odd prickle in the back of my throat. I mean, I knew it was safe and that if I popped some molly I'd have an awesome time—a time that might even make up for my last two-plus weeks of incarceration—but I'd promised my dad. He was trusting me. Maybe we shouldn't have left Jess's house after all.

Kelly spotted us from across the pool and came running over. She gave Jess a big, fat kiss and then threw her arms around me yelling that she thought she'd never see me again. Then she dragged us both into the plush basement and over to the bar, where a guy with spiky green hair was cutting molly.

You guys are in, right? Say you're in! Kelly cheered.

There was a mirror over the bar and I caught a glimpse of two old people on the couch behind us. I flinched around. They weren't crazy, grandparent old, but they were at least my parents' age. And they were sitting on the couch in bathing suits, sliding their hands up and down each other's bare legs and arms, their eyes wide and unfocused like they were in ecstasy.

I thought you said her parents weren't going to be here, I said, totally freaked.

Oh, those aren't her parents. That dude is Jasmine's supplier, and I guess that's his girlfriend or whatever, Kelly said. His shit is good.

The two adults started making out, him pressing her back onto the couch. Something about those two going at it made me sick to my stomach, but I also couldn't look away. It was kind of like a train wreck. The first time I'd been out of my house and away from my warden parents and all I could think about was getting out of here and going home.

You want? The green-haired guy asked, holding out a tiny, expertly prepared bag of molly to me. Jess and Kelly were already holding theirs. I looked in the mirror. The man was untying his girlfriend's bathing suit.

Yeah. I want.

I took the bag and downed it with an entire bottle of water, then grabbed my friends' arms and pulled them back outside. No way did I want to watch the over-the-hill sex show anymore. I dove right into the pool and let the cool water envelop me. It felt so good I suddenly realized I probably could have gone without the drugs. Everything felt good to me after being locked up. Just breathing the fresh air, feeling the sun on my face, hearing my friends' voices. But it was too late now. The drugs were already working their way into my system. And before long, I started to feel them. At one point, I emerged from the water and there was a crazy glow around the sun. I knew I was rolling.

I got out of the pool and found a towel, which I laid down on the grass, letting the warmth of the sun coat my body. My skin tingled everywhere, and suddenly I wished like anything that Carson was there, but my parents hadn't given me back my phone, so I couldn't even text him to come over. I lifted my head to look around for Jess, and realized she was right beside me, making out with Kelly like a madwoman. I laughed and lay back down again. Huge bubbles floated past my face, making rainbows across the sky. I'd never seen anything so beautiful.

Before long I felt someone caressing the skin on my arm, and it felt sooo good. I looked over, and it was Kelly. She was still making out with Jess, but she was stroking my arm. I laughed, wondering if she even realized she was touching the wrong girl. Then she kind of rolled off Jess and cuddled up next to me, saying my skin was so soft. She kissed my neck, and it felt so good just to be touched. Before I knew it, Jess was kissing my neck on the other side. I kept giggling, and they kind of made a game of it, seeing who could make me laugh the hardest. Then they sat up again and started kissing each other right over me, making a bridge over my belly. I watched them, and Jess's hair trailed on my skin, setting every particle on fire. After a while I closed my eyes, and they eventually went back to toying with my skin, playing with my fingers and toes like I was their personal toy. It was fun and silly and chill, and every moment of it felt so very good.

Now, as I'm writing this, I'm glad that's as far as it went. I know from experience how things can get out of control, and I love Jess, but I don't want to kiss her on the mouth or do anything else like that with her. I think it would mess with our friendship. It's a little weird that she was kissing my neck, I guess, but not really. I've done more than that with other girls.

The two things that are freaking me out are: 1) the fact that I lied straight to my father's face when I got home tonight. I made up this whole story about how we ordered pizza and watched old videos of us from when we were little. I don't even know where all the details came from, but they just did, and he believed me.

No drugs? he said.

No drugs, I told him.

I didn't even blink. And every time I think about it, I feel icky and twisted inside. But why? I just totally proved my point. I can do molly and be totally fine and not let things get out of hand. I can do it and then come home and be totally normal. So why do I feel like I've done something really, really wrong?

2) I can't get that older couple out of my head. They were my parents' age, yet they thought it was perfectly cool to spend

a summer Saturday rolling with a bunch of teenagers. I keep imagining that it was my parents, and every time I do, I start to heave. I wonder if they have kids. I wonder if their kids knew what they were doing today.

Every time I think about it, I shudder. Honestly, those people may have ruined molly for me. Ugh.

Sunday, July 27

Oh my god, Carson is here! We're going out to dinner! I can't believe he talked my parents into it, but he did! He kept saying, Just dinner, I swear. He apologized up and down about the Flaming Daisy Carnival and even told them he really cared about me and wouldn't let anything happen to me. My parents said it was fine, but I have to text them every half hour and update them on where we are and what we're doing. Ugh. But whatever. I'll do anything to spend a night with Carson. I feel like my life is finally getting back to normal. Okay, I have to go. Just wanted to write quickly how HAPPY I AM!!!!!

Monday, July 28

OMG, it hurts. . . . It hurts, and they won't tell me where Carson is. I can't I can't I can't.

Tuesday, July 29

Carson is in a coma. They won't let me see him. I'm on some kind of psychiatric hold in the hospital. My mom says they're worried I might try to kill myself.

I don't even know where to start.

Carson and I went out to Aldo's, that Italian restaurant where my dad takes my mom on their anniversary. It was so nice I felt out of place, even in my good black skirt. But it didn't matter, because Carson was wearing a blue jacket and a white shirt looking like he was going to the Grammys or something. His beauty totally made up for my lack thereof. He broke the ice with the waiter when he ordered a bottle of their finest cola, and after that, I relaxed. It was just so nice to be out. To be with him. To see him again. I felt like the last few weeks had been some horrible nightmare and now I was back where I should be.

Then he got a text. He looked at it and put it back in his pocket. I asked who it was, but he wouldn't tell me. He got another one, and I started to get suspicious. Was he seeing someone else? I felt hot all around my neck and under my arms. When the third text came in, he said he'd turn his phone off, but I made him show me the phone. All the texts were from Reid. He was at a party and wanted us to come. You've never seen so much good shit, the text said. With four exclamation points.

The shit he was referring to, of course, was drugs.

My mouth actually started to water. The party with Jess and Kelly was a little weird with the parental rollers and all, but I wanted to do molly with Carson again. I knew that if I did, it would make the icky feeling from yesterday go away.

Let's go, I said to Carson. He said no way. He told me tonight was just about being with me, and he didn't want to betray my parents' trust. I laughed. Screw my parents. They had kept me locked in my room like a caged animal for DAYS. And if he wanted to be with me, why not be with me on molly so we could really relax? It took a lot of convincing, but finally he said okay. Anything for you, he said.

Oh, god. It kills me now, just writing that. Anything for me. We'd gone there for me. It was my idea. I'd pushed it. And now . . . . Oh my god, what if he doesn't wake up? What if he . . .

I can't.

Okay, so I grinned and kissed him right there over our pasta dishes. I texted my parents that we were about to order our second course, and Carson asked for the check.

The party was in the woods off the hiking trail where dad used to take us as kids. There were dozens of people there, and everyone was completely high by the time we arrived. Reid was jumping up and down and bouncing around like a jumping bean. He'd taken off his T-shirt and tied it around his head. When he saw us, he threw his arms around us and kissed us both on the mouth. He tasted like beer and tuna fish.

Carson just laughed. Reid's pupils almost covered the blue in his eyes. My skin prickled. I wanted to feel as good as he did, though hopefully not look as stupid.

Where's the molly? I asked.

Reid dragged us over to this guy sitting at the base of a huge oak tree. Two girls were lying next to him, one with her head on his thigh while he turned the other way and put together pouches of molly. He was big and really fat and he had a black leather vest on over a white T-shirt that was stained and rising up to expose his belly. For a split second everything felt wrong. Who was this guy? We didn't know if his molly was safe, and there was no one here to test it. But then, all of a sudden, Carson shouted, Is that Big Dave?!

The guy looked up and smiled, and the two of them slapped hands. Carson told me that Big Dave used to coach his little league soccer team and still lives down the street from his house. I relaxed a little after that. If Carson knew him, he couldn't be a bad guy.

Big Dave handed us pouches of molly and bottled water. Carson paid him. When he handed the money over, Dave held his hand for an extra minute, and I could tell he was passing Carson something. I should have asked what it was, but I didn't. I didn't want to sound like the drug police or something. Besides, all I could think about was getting high as fast as possible because the party was crazy. People were half dressed and moshing, and there was a fire in the middle of the clearing. It all looked vaguely *Lord of the Flies*-ish, and I had a feeling it would be a lot more enjoyable once the molly kicked in.

Which it was. Carson and I were slow dancing in the middle of all the crazies when I felt my brain go light and the flames of the fire went blue and purple and green. I leaned my head against his chest and heard his heart pounding over the electronic drums in the music. He buried his hands in my hair and massaged my head and the feeling of my own hair rubbing my scalp was like a million fingers tickling my skin. When he tipped my head back and kissed me, it was like our lips were exploding together into a million prickling particles of energy.

I saw Carson down a second hit of molly and asked if he had more. He gave me another, and after that everything just got more and more intense. Suddenly I started feeling jittery. It was like my whole body was vibrating. Someone slammed into me from behind. I shoved back, and shoving felt good. It felt, for a second, like the crazy energy inside of me had a release. But then, it was back. My jaw clenched and my eyes were shaking.

Someone knocked me from behind, and I rammed my shoulder into their back. Then someone else shoved me, and I hit the ground on my ass. I looked up, and all I saw were flailing limbs and closed eyes and fire. Then I saw Carson, downing another hit of molly.

Someone stepped on my hand, and my fingers exploded in pain. Fear coursed through me, hot and feral and alive. I shoved myself up. The dancers around me had red eyes. They had fangs. They were painted with blood. I turned around to find Carson, and he grabbed me roughly, locking one hand around the back of my head and shoving his tongue so far into my mouth I thought I was going to choke.

I was high. Very, very high. But I still knew this wasn't right. I shoved him off of me. He shoved me back. Hard. The back of my head slammed into the tree behind me. Carson laughed and took a fourth hit of molly, downing it with an entire bottle of water. He chugged it so fast, the water streamed down the side of his face and dripped onto his bare shoulders. When had he taken his shirt off? The water glistened like blood.

I grabbed his arm. The back of my head throbbed, and when I touched it with my free hand, it felt wet. I was bleeding. Carson! We have to get out of here!

The music was so loud, it was pounding inside my chest.

Carson flung me off of him. You're the one who wanted to come here!

That was the last thing he said to me—You're the one who wanted to come here.

He cackled and then turned around and ran. He sprinted around the party clearing in a circle, cheering and jumping and then running some more. He and Reid slammed chests, then both fell back on the ground, and were up again in an instant. I backed away from the other partiers, taking shelter under a tree as the world started to spin. My jaw was so tight, my temples hurt. I needed some gum or something to eat, but I didn't know anyone and I could barely make sense of what I was seeing.

The next time Carson breezed past me, I grabbed his wrist.

We need to go.

Carson stopped. He looked at me and for a split second, his eyes focused. Oh, thank god, I thought. Maybe it wasn't as bad as I thought. Maybe this stuff was harsh but went through your system fast, and he was already coming down. I gripped both his hands, waiting for him to say, Yeah. Let's get out of here.

Then his eyes rolled into the back of his head. He went down so fast, I didn't even have time to scream. His skull slammed into a rock and one of the dancing psychos stepped fully on his face with his huge sneaker. Blood seeped out of

Carson's nose, but he didn't move. He didn't twitch or writhe or anything. He was gone.

That was when I started to scream.

Later . . .

The doctor just told me I'm lucky to be alive. I don't feel lucky. I feel like shit. I couldn't write anymore after that last bit. My dad says Carson is still comatose. He says maybe I can see him tomorrow. All I can think about is how handsome he looked at the restaurant. How he wanted to stay. How right now he would be home and safe if I'd just let him stay.

I don't even remember how we got out of the woods. I just remember a lot of people running and me screaming into a phone and then flashing lights. I think I passed out after that. I remember flying down a hallway on a stretcher, my mom's purse slapping against my arm. And I remember the stomach pumping. I will NEVER forget that. When some big male nurse shoves a tube down your throat and you wretch all over yourself, it's not something you forget, even if you want to. The inside of my throat still hurts, and all I can eat is broth and Jell-O.

There was some kind of chemical in the molly. Something that makes it hit you faster, but can also cause bad reactions.

Fucking Big Dave. I told the cops exactly where they could find that troll. I hope he goes to jail for life.

I just wish they'd let me see Carson. Maybe if he could hear my voice, he'd wake up. I just want to look him in the eye and tell him I'm sorry and that I will never, ever make him go to a party again. I just want to tell him I love him.

Wednesday, July 30

I'm home. Everyone's tiptoeing around me like they think I'm going to explode. Exploding is the last thing I feel like doing. I feel like curling up in a ball and dying. Slowly. And as painfully as possible.

They let me see Carson today before we checked out of the hospital. I almost wish they hadn't, even after all my begging. He had this big tube sticking out of his mouth and a bandage on his nose. That jackass broke it when he stepped on him. He looked so pale, he was almost green, and even though it's only been a few days, he looked skinny. Shrunken. It was like his perfect, strong chest had gone concave.

His parents left me alone with him so I could talk to him, but when I opened my mouth, I just started sobbing. I clung to his hand and cried and cried and cried. When I finally could talk, I just kept saying I'm sorry over and over again. I wanted to say something encouraging. Tell him he was going to get better and that I'd be here when he did, but looking at him made it all seem impossible.

I don't think he's going to get better. But he has to. He has to. He's Carson. He's healthy and athletic and sweet and fun and kind and loving. He's going to college in the fall. His life is going to be perfect.

It has to be. It has to.

Friday, August 1

Jess came by today. I didn't want to talk to her. I don't want to talk to anyone. I was staring at the TV when she came in. She told me she wished she'd been there so she could have helped, but I didn't say anything. I'm glad she wasn't there. If she was, maybe she'd be in a coma too. Or dead.

I love Carson so much it hurts. I miss him so much, and I'm so, so scared. I can't think about anything else. I can't talk to anyone because I'll just start crying. He's the only person I want to talk to, and I won't talk again until I can talk to him.

Eventually, Jess gave up trying to talk to me and just sat there and watched TV in silence. I kept wishing she'd go away. When she finally did, I felt relieved.

Saturday, August 2

Carson is brain dead. My dad just told me. His parents are deciding whether or not to keep him on the machines. If they take him off, he'll die. He'll die. He's going to die.

Monday, August 4

It's my fault. It's my fault. It's all my fault. I'm never going to hear him laugh again. I'm never going to hear him say my name, see him smile, touch his face. He's never going to go to college or play soccer or get married or have kids. And it's all my fault. Mine. You're the one who wanted to come here, he said. And he was right. I made him go to the party. I made him leave the restaurant. All he wanted to do was sit with me and eat dinner and talk. That was what he wanted. And I killed him.

Friday, August 8

Carson is gone. His funeral is tomorrow. I can't go. I can't face all those people. They know what I did. They know it was me. I wish they'd put me in the ground with him.

Monday, August 11

My mother took me to see Tim today. I cried the entire time. Just sat on his couch and cried. He gave me a box of tissues, and

I used the whole thing. Everything hurts. Every last inch of me. He kept saying, Tell me what you're feeling. What are you feeling right now?

I told him I want to die.

Wednesday, August 13

Someone has been sitting by my bed at all times for the past two days. My mom, my dad, Ashley, Jess, Tim, even my grandmother is here. I haven't spoken to any of them. I don't know what they're doing. I don't know why they're here. I wish they would go away.

My mom keeps trying to make me eat, but I can't. I won't. Carson will never eat anything ever again. I wonder if he knew what was happening right before he passed out. I wonder if he was scared. I wonder if he hated me, in that moment. If that was why he looked at me so clearly right before he went down. Because he knew. He knew that his life was over and it was my fault.

Friday, August 15

Apparently I slept for two days and while I was sleeping, my mom read this journal. I woke up and she was sitting in front of me, crying, with the journal open in her lap. I sat up to shout at her, and my brain went fuzzy so fast I had to lay right down again. The room was spinning. I closed my eyes and brought my hands to my head, but it didn't help. I could feel the bed underneath me turning, my organs fighting to keep up with the constant motion.

Mommy, make it stop, I heard myself say.

She gently moved my hands and kissed my forehead. I'd never felt anything so good.

That's all I want to do, she said.

I can't believe she read the whole thing. I can't believe she knows everything. All the sex and the drugs and the insanity. I can't believe she still kissed me after reading all that. OMG, I think I'm going to throw up.

Later . . .

Tonight my dad brought me chicken broth in a mug with a lid and a little spout, so I wouldn't spill it, and said I had to drink it. I was offended at first. I'm not a baby. But when I tried to hold it, I was so weak I almost dropped it, so then I knew why. My mother and father sat on either side of my bed and watched me drink it. I felt like a prisoner again, but the warm liquid felt so good going down, I didn't care. Then my mother took out the journal and handed it to me. She told me she wanted me to read it, from beginning to end, and then she wanted me to decide what I wanted to do.

What does that mean? I asked.

Well, I guess it means do you want to live, or do you want to die?

Then they both left my room.

Saturday, August 16

I stayed up all night reading. If some of the pages in this thing are smeared, it's because I couldn't stop crying. I've never felt so many clashing emotions at the same time in my life. I felt stupid and angry and indignant and sad and happy and excited and terrified and guilty. Carson never needed the drugs, did he? He was always fine just being with me. He did them for fun, but he never needed them to feel comfortable or happy. I never thought of myself as the one pushing this on other people, but that's what I did to him and not just that last night. He wanted to be with ME. Not the me I was on molly. He loved me. He really loved me. I'll never forgive myself for what I did to him. Never.

Sunday, August 17

I just got into a screaming fight with Jess. I woke up and she was sitting in a chair, watching me. I asked her why she was here, and she said, You're on suicide watch.

So? Wasn't it my family's job to watch me? What the hell was she doing here?

I asked her again, and she freaked out. She said, I care about you, you asshole! I love you! You're my best friend, and I'm not going to let you die!

So, I told her she'd be better off without me. I apparently kill the people I love.

And she said I did not kill Carson. It was Carson's decision to do drugs. His decision to take four hits. And it was Big Dave's decision to cut some crazy shit into the molly. If Carson was here, he'd tell you the exact same thing! YOU DID NOT KILL ANYONE! she screamed at me. GET OVER YOURSELF, AND GET THE HELL OUT OF BED!

Then she stormed out of my room, and slammed the door.

Tonight, when my mom brought me toast, I ate it. I almost threw it up, but I managed to keep it down. I kept telling myself just one more bite. Just get through one more bite. Then you can sleep.

Monday, August 18

I can't stop thinking about what Jess said about getting over myself. I read through this journal again today, and I realized everything in it is about me. I mean, it's supposed to be about my life and everything, but so much of it is about what other people are thinking of me. What they do to me. How they make me feel. Whether they like me or think I'm pretty or dorky or what. It's like . . .

It's like I never think about anybody else, or how they feel, or what they need or want. I swear there's something wrong with me. I don't want to be that person. I don't. I feel so fucking stupid.

Jess is right. I have to get over myself. But it's just so hard. Everything feels so hard.

Wednesday, August 20

Today my dad took off work to go to Tim's with me and my mom and Ashley. I told them all I wanted them to be there, but when I sat down on the couch, my throat closed over. I felt like an idiot for thinking I could do this. I felt like an asshole for putting them through what I'd put them through. I felt like a huge, stinking hypocrite, junkie loser. But even though I knew I was wrong, it was SO hard to say it. SO FUCKING HARD. I hated the idea that they would all be thinking I told you so. That they would all feel so vindicated. But I knew what I had to do if I wanted to change. If I wanted to stop feeling like such shit and making the people around me feel like such shit.

I loved Carson. I did. But I didn't want to end up like him.

I was wearing a sweatshirt, and I wound the cord around and around and around my finger until there was no blood left in the tip.

Take your time, Tim said.

I opened my mouth and tears filled my eyes. One, big, fat drop hit my knee. I looked up at my mom, but I could barely see her through all the blur.

I decided, I said and choked on a sob.

Decided what, honey? my mom asked.

I breathed in.

I decided I want to live.

Some parties just don't end well . . .

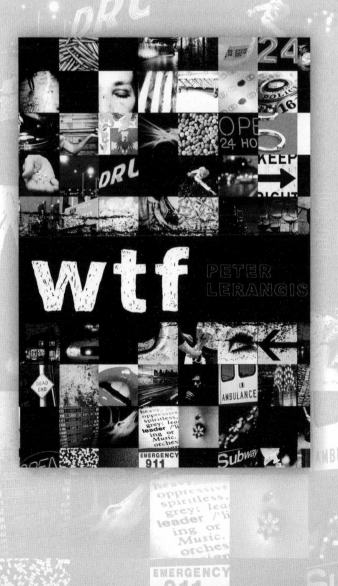

JIMMY
October 17, 9:07 P.M.

The eyes were beautiful.

They were mad huge, anime-hero huge, staring out of the darkness.

Something brushed his cheek too, rhythmically. Like kisses.

Jimmy smiled.

Kisses happened all the time to guys like Cam, who expected them. Never to Jimmy.

So he would always remember that moment, how weirdly tender and exciting it was on that deserted road on that rainy October evening, before he blinked and realized his world had gone to shit.

9:08 P.M.

It wasn't the taste of blood that brought him to reality. Or the rain pelting his face through the jagged shark-jaw where the windshield had been. Or the car engine, screaming like a vacuum cleaner on steroids. Or the glass in his teeth.

It was the sight of Cam's feet.

They were thick, forceful feet, Sasquatch feet whose size you knew because Cam bragged about it all the time (14EE), feet that seemed to be their own form of animal life. But right now, in a pool of dim light just below the passenger seat, they looked weightless and demure, curved like a ballerina's. One flip-flop had fallen off, but both legs were moving listlessly with the rhythm of the black mass that lay across the top half of Cam's body—the mass that was attached to the eyes that were staring up at Jimmy.

"Shit!"

Jimmy lurched away. The animal was twitching, smacking its nose against his right arm now, flinging something foamy and warm all over the car. It was half in and half out, its hindquarters resting on the frame of the busted windshield, its haunches reaching out over the hood. The broken remains of a mounted handheld GPS device hung from the dash like an incompletely yanked tooth.

For a moment he imagined he was home, head down on his desk, his mom nudging him awake with a cup of hot cocoa. It was Friday night. He was always home on Friday night. But this was real, and he remembered now— the deer springing out of the darkness, running across the road, legs pumping, neck strained. . . .

"CAAAAAM! BYRON!"

His voice sounded dull, muffled by the rain's ratatat-ting on the roof. No one answered. Not Byron in the back-seat.

Not Cam.

Cam.

Was he alive? He wasn't crying out. Wasn't saying a thing.

Jimmy fumbled for the door handle. His fingers were

cold and numb. With each movement the engine screamed, and he realized his right foot was stuck against the accelerator, trapped between it and a collapsed dashboard. He tried to pull it out and squeeze the door handle, but both were stuck. He gave up on his foot and looked for the lock.

There.

The door fell open with a metallic *grrrrrock*. Jimmy hung on to the armrest, swinging out with the door, as a red pickup sped by. It swerved to avoid him, and Jimmy tried to shout for help. His foot still stuck, he spilled out headfirst, twisting so his shoulders hit the pavement. As his teeth snapped shut, blood oozed over his bottom lip. He spat tiny glass particles.

The pickup was racing away, past a distant streetlight, which cast everything in a dim, smoky glow. From the car's windshield, the deer's hind legs kicked desperately in silhouette, like the arms of a skinny cheerleader pumping a victory gesture.

As Jimmy yanked his own leg, not caring if the fucking thing came off at the ankle, he felt the rain washing away the blood. Through the downpour he could see the long, furry face on the seat—nodding, nodding, as if in sympathy. *That's it, pal. Go. Go. Go.*

His ankle pulled loose, and he tumbled backward

onto the road, legs arcing over his head. As he lay still, catching his breath, he heard someone laugh, a desperate, high-pitched sound piercing the rain's din.

It took a moment before he realized it was his own voice.

9:09 P.M.

"Jesus, it's still alive!"

Byron's voice. From the backseat.

Byron was okay.

Jimmy jumped up from the road. He struggled to keep upright, his leg numb. He spat his mouth clean as he made his way around the car. Through the side window he could see Byron's silhouette, peering over the front seat. Jimmy looked through the driver's side window. The deer's back was enormous, matted with blood and flecks of windshield. Under it he could make out only the right side of Cam's body from the shoulder down, but not his face.

Cam was completely smothered.

"Oh God, Jimmy, what did you do?" Byron said.

"I—I don't know. . . . It just, like, *appeared*!" Jimmy

had to grip the side of the car to keep from falling, or flying away, or completely disintegrating. He blinked, trying desperately to find the right angle, hoping to see a sign that Cam was alive. "Push it, Byron—push it off!"

"It's a monster—how the fuck am I supposed to push it? *Shit, Jimmy, how could you have not seen it?*"

"*I did!*" Jimmy screamed. "I braked. I tried to get out of the way—"

"Dickwad! You tried to outmaneuver a *deer*? You don't *brake*! That makes the grill drop lower—lifts the animal right up into the car, like a fucking spoon! You just *drive*. That way you smack it right back into the woods."

"*If you know so much, why weren't you driving?*"

"With what license?"

"*I don't have one either!*"

"You told me you did!"

"I never told you that! I just said I knew how to drive. I never took the test—"

"Oh, great—the only person in Manhattan our age who knows how to drive, *and you don't bother to get a license.*" Byron leaned closer, suddenly looking concerned. "Jesus Christ, what happened to your mouth?"

"It's what I get for applying lipstick without a mirror—"

"Awwww, *shit*!" Byron was looking at something in his hand. "My BlackBerry's totaled."

"How can you think about your BlackBerry while Cam is under the deer?"

Byron looked up with a start, then immediately leaped out of the car. "Oh fuck, Cam. Is he dead?"

"*'Oh fuck, Cam'*? You just noticed him? You're yelling at me, and you just thought of Cam?" Jimmy's hands trembled as he pulled his cell phone out of his pocket. "I'm calling 911."

"No, don't!" Byron said, snatching the phone from Jimmy's hand.

"Are you crazy?" Jimmy said. "What's wrong with you?"

"We're in East Dogshit and the GPS is busted—do you even know what road we're on? What are you going to tell the cops? *Um, there's this tree? And, like, a ditch? And a road*? And then what, we wait? We don't have time, Jimmy!"

"But—"

"Think it through, Einstein. What's your story? One, you wrecked a car that's not yours. Two, you don't have a license. Three, you killed a deer. And four, look at Cam. You planning to go to Princeton and room with Rhodes scholars? How about a guy with three teeth who can't wait for you to bend over? Because if we don't stop talking, dude, you're facing murder charges."

"He's not dead, Byron—"

"Just put the fucking phone away and let's get Bambi off Cam." Byron threw Jimmy the phone and raced to the back of the car. "Throw me the keys. I'll get a rope out of the trunk. When I give you back the keys, get in the car."

Jimmy reached into the car, tossing the phone onto the dashboard. Quickly removing the keys from the steering column, he threw them to Byron. He eyed the driver's seat. The deer was still moving, still trying to get away. *No way* was he going back in there.

But he couldn't abandon Cam.

If only he could think straight. His brain was useless. In that moment, he was picturing a cloud of small, hungry ticks hovering over the front seat. He tried to shake it off, but it was like some weird psychological hijacking brought on by his mother's lifelong vigil over the mortal threat posed by proximity to deer, which turned every suburban outing into a preparation for war.

"What are you fucking worried about, Lyme's disease?" Byron shouted. "Get in there!"

Jimmy cringed. "It's *Lyme*," he muttered, grabbing the door handle. "Not *Lyme's*."

"What?" Byron shouted.

"Nothing. What am I supposed to do—in the car?"

"What the fuck do you think you're supposed to do?"

As if in response, the deer gave a sudden shudder. Jimmy jumped back, stifling a scream. "I—I'm not sure . . ."

"When I give the word, put it in reverse, Jimmy. And gun it."

Byron yanked open the trunk and threw the keys to Jimmy, who kept a wary eye on the deer as he opened the door. It was motionless now, its snout resting just below the gear shift.

As Jimmy climbed inside, the car rocked with Byron's efforts to shove stuff under the rear tires for traction.

Breathe in. Breathe out.

Jimmy tried to stop himself from hyperventilating. He eyed Cam's feet, blinking back tears. He had never liked Cam, or any of the smart-ass jocks who treated the Speech Team kids like they were some kind of lower life-form. Since freshman year he had devoted a lot of time conjuring horrible fates for most of them, fates not unlike this.

In . . . Out . . .

Jimmy hadn't wanted to go on this drive. It was Byron who'd pushed the idea. *Cam* wants us to go, *Cam* says suburban parties are the best ever, *Cam* says Westchester chicks are hot for NYC guys. *Cam* wants to be friends. It would be stupid to miss a chance at détente between the worlds of sports and geekdom.

In . . .

Until this time, Jimmy couldn't imagine that Byron would be friends with a guy like Cam. Byron the potty-mouthed genius, Cam the football guy. Was this some kind of crush? Was *that* the reason for—

"Wake up, douche bag!" Byron shouted. "Now! *Go!*"

With his foot on the brake, Jimmy threw the car in reverse. The accelerator was touching the bottom of the caved-in dashboard. Carefully, he wedged his foot in and floored it.

The engine roared to life, the tires gripping the debris. As the car lurched backward, the deer's head rose slowly off the seat with the force of the rope. Something warm spattered against the side of Jimmy's face.

"AAAGHH!" he screamed, yanking his foot away from the accelerator.

"*WHAT?*" Byron cried, running around the side of the car. "Why'd you stop? We almost had it!"

"It puked on me!"

Byron shone a flashlight into the front seat. "It's not puke. It's blood."

"Oh, great . . ." Jimmy's stomach flipped. *This couldn't be happening!*

"Here. This'll protect you." Byron was throwing something over the animal's head—a rag, a blanket, it was impossible to see. "Don't think about it, Jimmy. Just step on it! And put on your seat belt."

Jimmy felt a lightness in his head. His eyes were crossing. *Focus.*

He buckled his belt and put the car in reverse again, slipping his foot under the wreckage of the dashboard. As he floored it, the car began to move, the engine roaring. The animal's hulk rose up beside him, away from him—scraping across the bottom of the windshield, slowly receding out of the car and onto the hood.

The blanket fell off the deer's head, as the carcass finally slipped off, the car jerked backward.

SMMMMACK!

Jimmy's head whipped against the headrest. He bounced back, his chest catching the seat belt and knocking the wind out of him.

"Are you okay?" Byron cried.

"Fah—fah—" Everything was white. Jimmy struggled to breathe, his eyes slowly focusing on the image in the rearview mirror, the twisted metal of a guardrail reflecting against the taillights.

Byron was leaning in the open passenger window, training a flashlight on the dim silhouette of Cam's lifeless body, now freed from the deer. "This does not look good. . . ." he said.

"Is his chest moving?"

"I don't know! I don't think so, but I can't—" In the distance a muffled siren burst through the rain's din. Byron drew back, shutting the flashlight. "Shit! Did you call them?"

"No!" Jimmy said.

"Then how do they know?"

Jimmy thought about the red pickup. "Someone drove past us, just after the accident. Maybe they called."

"Someone saw us?"

"This is a New York suburb. Occasionally people drive on the roads."

"Oh, God. Oh, God. Oh, God. Oh, shit. Oh, God." Byron was backing away from the car, disappearing into the darkness.

"I'm the one who's supposed to be freaking out, not you!" Jimmy leaned toward Cam's inert body, his hands

shaking. The cold rain, evaporating against his body, rose up in smoky wisps. *Don't be dead don't be dead please please please please don't be dead.*

"C-C-Cam?" Jimmy slapped Cam's cheek and shook his massive shoulders, but Cam was limp and unresponsive. His body began to slip on the rain-slicked seat, falling toward the driver's side. Jimmy tried to shove back, but he was helpless against the weight. Cam's head plopped heavily in Jimmy's lap.

"Aaaaghhh!" He pushed open the door, jumped out, and looked around for Byron. "I think he's . . . he's . . ."

The siren's wail was growing closer. How would he explain this? *You see, officer, in New York City no one gets a license until they're in college. But my dad taught me to drive on weekends, on Long Island. No, I don't have the registration either. The car belongs to—belonged to . . . him . . . the deceased.*

He'd have to get out of here before they came. He looked past the car. There was a gully, a hill. It was pitch-black. He could get lost in the night.

Asshole! No, the cops would figure it out. Fingerprints. Friends knew he was driving—Reina Sanchez, she had to know. She was all over Cam. She'd tell them. So it wouldn't only be manslaughter. It would also be leaving the scene of the crime. What was that? Life in prison?

Stay or go, he was screwed either way. Because of a deer. A fucking stupid deer. Without the deer, everything would have been all right.

"BYRON!" he shouted.

In the distance he heard Byron retching, with characteristic heroism.

Cam was now slumped into the driver's seat, his right shoulder touching the bottom of the steering wheel.

He used me. He convinced Byron to get me to drive so he could go to a party. And now he will never ever be accountable. Because he's . . .

Dead. He was dead. He would never move again, never talk.

And that opened up several possibilities, some of which were

Unthinkable.

An idea was taking shape cancerously fast among his battered brain cells. If you were thinking something, it wasn't unthinkable—that was Goethe, or maybe Wittgenstein, or Charlie Brown. The idea danced between the synapses, on the line between survival and absolute awfulness, presenting itself in a sick, Quentin Tarantino way that made perfect sense.

It was Cam's dad's car. It would be logical that Cam would be driving it.

No one will know.

He grabbed Cam's legs. They were heavy, dead weight. He pulled them across the car toward the driver's side, letting Cam's butt slide with them—across the bench seat, across the pool of animal blood and pebbled glass.

Jimmy lifted Cam into an upright position, but his body fell forward, his torso resting hard against the steering wheel.

HONNNNNNNNNNNK!

The sound was ridiculously loud. Around the bend, distant headlights were making the curtain of rain glow. No time to fix this now.

Jimmy bolted for the woods.

"What are you doing?" Byron called out of the dark. He was standing now, peering into the car. "Jesus Christ! You're trying to *make it look like Cam drove*? What if he's alive? He'll tell them you were driving!"

Jimmy stopped, frantically looking around for something blunt. He stooped to pick up a rusted piece of tailpipe, maybe a foot long. It would do the trick. He knelt by the driver's door and drew it back.

"JIMMY, ARE YOU OUT OF YOUR FUCKING MIND?"

Byron's eyes were like softballs. He grabbed Jimmy's arm.

Jimmy let the tailpipe fall to the ground. He felt his brain whirling, his knees buckling. He felt Byron pulling him away.

As the cop cars squealed to a halt near the blaring car, he was moving fast but feeling nothing.

Making the right choice
is never easy . . .
Lucy in the Sky

IN THE TRADITION OF *GO ASK ALICE*

Lucy in the Sky

Anonymous

One party. One taste.
No turning back.

July 4

~~Dear Diary,~~

That's ridiculous. Who writes "Dear Diary" in a diary? I mean, who writes in a diary at all? Shouldn't I be blogging?

This is lame.

July 5

Okay, so this isn't going to be a diary. It's a journal. I guess that's the same thing, but "journal" sounds less like I'm riding a tricycle or something.

Yesterday was my birthday. I turned 16.

It's so weird sharing a birthday with your country. Always fireworks: never for you. Mom always plans an actual birthday dinner—usually the Saturday night after July 4th so that I can have a day where we celebrate just for me. It's fun, kinda like having two birthdays in the same week.

We're not big July 4th celebrators . . . celebrators? Celebrants? People. Whatever—we're not big on July 4th. Usually in the afternoon we have friends from school over and walk down to the beach to play volleyball. There are lots of nets at the beach just down the hill, then we haul ourselves back up the canyon to our house for a cookout in the evening. My brother, Cam, invites his friends from the varsity soccer team. Mom gets my favorite cake (the one with the berries in it).

After we gorge on grilled meat and birthday cake, we all crowd onto the balcony outside my parents' bedroom and watch the fireworks down the coast. You can see the display at the pier really well, and the ones in the cities just up the coast shoot off too. Last year Cam (nobody calls him Cameron except Mom) climbed onto the roof from the front porch so he could get a better view, but Mom freaked and said, CAMERON! Get. Down. This. Instant. Mom's big on safety.

I got a lot of cool presents yesterday. Mom got me the swimsuit I tried on at the mall last week. It's a really cute two-piece with boy shorts, and this fun, twisty top. Dad's present to me was that he's taking me to get my license this week. I've been practicing with him in the parking lot near his office at the college. He gave me a coupon for one "Full Day with Dad." On the back it says, "Good for one driving test at the DMV, followed by a celebratory meal at the restaurant of holder's choosing, and a $100 shopping spree/gift card to store of choice."

He made it himself out of red construction paper and drew this funny little stick figure on the front. It's supposed to be him. He draws curly hair on the sides of the round head so the little man is bald on top like he is. The coupon is sort of cheesy, but so is my dad. I think it's funny. And cute.

Cam got me this journal. We've been going to this yoga

class together, and the teacher is this woman named Marty with bright eyes who talks about her birds a lot. She told us to get a journal and spend a few minutes each day writing down our thoughts and feelings.

I just looked back at everything I've written, and it's mainly thoughts. Not very many feelings. I'm not sure how I feel right now. I mean, I guess I feel fine? Happy?

No, just fine. I feel fine.

I also feel like people who have birds are sort of weird.

July 6

It's funny that Cam bought me this journal. It's one of those things I would never have bought for myself but secretly wanted. I don't know how he knows that stuff. I guess that's what older brothers are supposed to do: read your mind. I mean, who actually goes out and tries the stuff that their yoga teacher says to do outside of class?

Cam got way into yoga last summer when he had a crush on this exchange student from England named Briony—like Brian with a y. (Really? Who names their kid that?) Anyway, she wouldn't give Cam the time of day, so when he found out that she went to this yoga class, he started going to the same one. He bought a mat and this little bag to carry it in and just happened to show up in her class like, Oh my God! Wow!

What a coincidence. Briony never went out with him. I didn't even know she'd gone back to London until I was teasing him about how he should be glad Briony didn't do something like synchronized swimming. He was like, Briony moved back to London right after school got out.

I asked him why he was still going to yoga, and he said he really liked it. And he said I should come.

I'm not sure why I did, really. I guess I was just bored last summer. But now we go to yoga together. It's this really great studio a block off the Promenade, and they run it on donations. You just pay what you can or what you think the class is worth. I didn't think I'd like it at first. It was hard, and I got sweaty and slipped on my mat and couldn't do any of the poses. But I sorta like spending time with Cam.

Who am I writing that to? It's not like anyone is reading this but me. This is exactly how it feels when Grams asks me to pray over dinner. I feel like I'm saying all this stuff that is bouncing back at me off the ceiling and landing in the spinach salad.

Cam probably didn't have to read my mind about wanting a journal at all. He's really smart. His early acceptance letter to this great college up north came last week. He's going to be a biochem major, which just makes me want to lie down on the floor and curl up in a ball. He's a brainiac. And on top of it he's nice and enthusiastic—which has a tendency to be dangerous.

Last semester Mom was always telling me to ask Cam for help with my geometry homework. I did, but instead of telling me what to do, Cam always talks and talks and talks. It's like he knows so much about stuff and likes math so much that he has to say it all instead of just the answer.

I stopped asking questions. It sort of annoyed me. Just did it myself, and didn't really understand it. I got a C in geometry. You'd have thought I'd flown a plane into a building. (That's bad to say, I guess. I mean, I know people died and everything, but it was a really long time ago.)

Dad came unglued. He's the chairman of the music department at the college where he works. He made me sign up for tutoring this summer with a student that his friend in the math department recommended. Our session starts in a few minutes. I was relieved when Nathan showed up the first time. I was afraid I'd get stuck with some weird math girl.

Nathan is a freshman. He's from Nebraska and has brown hair that's cut short. He works out a lot, and he wears these polo shirts with sleeves that are tight right around his biceps. I just stare at his arms a lot instead of listening when he's trying to help me find the answer.

I wish somebody would just tell me the answer.

Nathan's here. Gotta go.

Later . . .

OMG.

I TOTALLY JUST INVITED NATHAN TO MY BIRTHDAY DINNER.

OMG OMG OMG OMG

And

He

Said

YES!

This is totally crazy. I can't believe I actually said the words out loud. I didn't mean to. We were just sitting at the dining room table and he was talking about the hypotenuse of a right angle, and while he was looking at the protractor he was using to draw lines, I was staring at the lines of his jaw and noticed that they were almost a right angle, and the hypotenuse of the right angle of his jaw was this line in his cheek with a dimple in the middle that he gets when he smiles, and then I heard myself saying, You should come to my birthday dinner on Saturday, and then I realized that Mom was looking RIGHT AT ME like my hair was on fire, and I realized that I'd just invited an 18-year-old over for dinner in FRONT OF MY MOTHER. OMG. I just wanted to CRAWL UNDER THE TABLE.

But he stopped with his pencil stuck into the protractor and looked up, and then glanced over at Mom like he was looking to see if she'd heard, and she smiled at him, sort of weakly. I guess he took that to mean that it was okay with her 'cause he looked me right in the eye and said, Sure. That'd be fun. Now look at this triangle.

I tried to look at the triangle for the rest of the half hour, but I have no idea what he was saying. When he left, I walked him to the door, and Mom said, Nathan, come by around 7:30. He said, Sure thing, and you can call me Nate. He waved at me before he got in his pickup truck and said, See you this weekend. Then, he drove away. Just like that.

I went running back up to my bedroom and buried my head in my pillow and did one of those silent screams where you just breathe out really hard, but with no sound; it's sort of a soft roar, but the excitement on the inside of me made it feel like my head would explode.

I could hear my heart pounding in my ears, and I took a couple of deep breaths and then I remembered what Marty said in yoga this morning about trying to meditate and how to focus on the breath, so I sat down on the floor and crossed my legs like Marty does in front of class, and I closed my eyes and took really deep breaths and tried not to think about Nate. I could do it for about 5 breaths at a time, but then I'd see that line with the dimple in it behind my eyelids, and then the rest of his right-angle jaw would appear and I'd see a triangle fill in the space on his face.

I mean, it's really no big deal. My dad is two years older than my mom. Nate's only 18, and I'm 16, and it's not like he would be robbing the cradle or anything.

I think I really like him.

OMG I CAN'T BELIEVE THAT NATE IS COMING TO DINNER ON SATURDAY.

July 8

I was just standing in my mirror trying on a couple of different options for tonight. I passed my driver's test and got my license yesterday (YAY! OMG. Finally!), then Dad and I went shopping on the Promenade. I'm a really good bargain shopper. Cam worked at the Gap last summer and taught me to never EVER pay full-price for anything 'cause they just mark it down every two weeks. Primary, secondary, clearance. Primary, secondary, clearance. Every week on Tuesday night the markdowns would come through from the home office, and we'd all run around with those price-tag guns the next morning, marking down tops that some poor dope had paid $20 more for 12 hours ago. So, anyway, I got a lot of great stuff. Even Dad was surprised with how many items I got for $100. Well, then I splurged a little and added $40 from my savings to get these supercute sandals that I'd been wanting.

Anyway, I have all this stuff to try on, and I felt myself doing that thing I do where I put on, like, 12 different outfits and stand there and pick every single one of them apart, and I end up standing in front of the mirror in my underwear with this pile of really cute clothes with the tags still on them lying on the floor. I had just put on the second skirt I bought and could tell I was about to find something wrong with it, and then I just stopped, looked at myself, and thought: Don't be that girl.

I just don't want to be that chick who is always staring at herself in the mirror whining about how she looks and having a meltdown in the fitting room. I mean, I'm not a model or anything, but I think I look okay. I have already showered and straightened my hair. It's not frizzy or even curly really—just has some waves, and when you live this close to the waves it can get wavy. (God. Stupid joke.) Whatever, I stepped away from the mirror and saw my journal sitting on my desk, and I thought I'd write about it. I mean, this is a feeling. I'm not sure what kinds of feelings I'm supposed to be writing about in here, but maybe this is what crazy Marty the bird lady was talking about.

I'm SO EXCITED about Nate coming over and I want to look really hot, but the excitement also feels like nervousness, like I'm going to barf or something. Mom is downstairs putting a marinade on some shrimp that she's going to have Dad grill, and the smell when I walked through the kitchen made me feel like I was going to hurl up my toenails—and I LOVE shrimp.

I know I look good in this skirt. Dad told me it looked "far out" when I came out of the dressing room to check it out in the mirror. He said this in his I'm-being-a-little-too-loud-so-the-other-people-present-will-hear-me-and-think-I'm-hilarious-when-really-I'm-just-torturing-my-daughter voice. I told him to please be quiet and offer his opinions only regarding possible escape routes in the case of a fire, or a random stampede of wild bison. In all other matters, I respectfully asked him to please refrain from speaking to me until we had reached the cash wrap.

I looked in the mirror again just now. This skirt totally works.

Weird how excited and scared feel like the same thing.

July 8—11:30 p.m.

I shoulda known.

I shoulda known when he walked up the front steps with flowers and handed them to Mom.

But he brought me a card with a joke about having pi on my birthday instead of cake (guh-rooooan) and it had a $25 gift card for iTunes in it. Which was cool and so sweet of him, but he just signed his name. Shoulda known when he didn't write anything personal. Just "Happy B-Day! Nate."

But he was really funny and sweet at dinner. He sat across from me and told us all this hilarious story about when he was growing up in Nebraska and he and his brother raised sheep for the county fair. (Yes. Apparently people still raise animals and take them to fairs where they win ribbons and titles and scholarships. Thank you, CHARLOTTE'S WEB.)

One morning he and his brother went out to scoop food out of these big 25-pound sacks of feed for the sheep, and there was a mouse in one of the bags that ran up his little brother's jacket sleeve. He was telling us about how he thought his brother had been possessed by a demon because he kept screaming and shaking his arms and beating at his chest and running around in a circle while the mouse wriggled around inside his shirt. We were all crying, we were laughing so hard, and Cam almost inhaled a bite of shrimp, which sent him on a coughing fit that made the rest of us laugh even harder.

He jumped up and helped me clear the table when Mom asked who wanted dessert. When Mom told him he didn't need to do that, he smiled at me and said, Oh yes, ma'am, I do. My mama'd fly in from Grand Island and smack me if I didn't.

When we were in the kitchen, I started rinsing plates and he loaded them into the dishwasher like he lived here. We were laughing and joking around and no one mentioned geometry.

He was so easy to talk to, easy to be near. I didn't feel nervous even once. I couldn't help but wonder what it would feel like if we were married and this was our house and we were loading the dishwasher together. That's probably stupid, but it made me feel hopeful inside, like maybe something like that was possible.

When Nate bent over to put the final plate in the dishwasher, a necklace fell out of his shirt. It had a tiny key on it, and I was about to ask him where he got it, but Mom came into the kitchen to get some coffee mugs and the French press. Nate tucked the necklace back into his polo before I could ask him about it, but I shoulda known.

There's a long porch on the back of our house that looks over the bottom of the canyon out to the water. We ate dessert out there. Dad lit the candles in the big lanterns on the table outside. Cam sat next to Nate and they talked soccer. The flicker made their skin glow like they were on the beach at sunset. Nate looked all sun-kissed and happy. I felt a foot nudge mine just for a second under the table and my heart started racing. I was glad that it was just the candles outside in the dark 'cause I started to blush like crazy. I thought maybe Nate had touched my foot, and I kept sliding mine a little bit closer toward him under the table, but his foot never touched mine again.

It was almost 10 when he pulled out his phone and checked it, then said, Whoa. I gotta go.